HATE THE GAME

WINTER RENSHAW

COPYRIGHT

COPYRIGHT 2019 WINTER RENSHAW
ALL RIGHTS RESERVED

COVER DESIGN: Louisa Maggio, LM Book Creations
EDITING: Wendy Chan, The Passionate Proofreader
BETA READER: Ashley Cestra
PHOTOGRAPHER: Wander Aguiar

All rights reserved. No part of this book may be reproduced or transmitted in any form, including electronic or mechanical, without written permission from the publisher, except in the case of brief quotations embodied in critical articles or reviews.

This is a work of fiction. Names, characters, places, and incidents either are the product of the author's imagination or, if an actual place, are used fictitiously and any resemblance to actual persons, living or dead, business establishments, events, or locales is entirely coincidental. The publisher does not have any control and does not assume any responsibility for author or third-party websites or their content.

E-Books are not transferrable. They cannot be sold, given away, or shared. The unauthorized reproduction or distribution of this copyrighted work is a crime punishable by law. No part of this book may be scanned, uploaded to or downloaded from file sharing sites, or distributed in any other way via the Internet or any other means, electronic or print, without the publisher's permission. Criminal copyright infringement, including infringement without monetary gain, is investigated by the FBI and is punishable by up to 5 years in federal prison and a fine of $250,000 (http://www.fbi.gov/ipr/).

This eBook is licensed for your personal enjoyment only. Thank you for respecting the author's work.

IMPORTANT

If you did not obtain this book via Amazon or Kindle Unlimited, it has been stolen. Downloading this book without paying for it is *against the law*, and often times those files have been *corrupted with viruses and malware* that can damage your reader or computer or steal your passwords and banking information. <u>Always obtain my books via Amazon and Amazon only</u>. Thank you for your support and for helping to combat piracy.

DESCRIPTION

Talon Gold is a lot of things: good at football, bad at love. Obsessed with scoring, refuses to play by the rules. Cruel. Relentless. Brilliant. Intoxicatingly attractive.

Despite his demanding reputation and propensity for being the most arrogant a-hole ever to strut Pacific Valley University's seaside campus, everyone wants a piece of him: coaches, scouts, and pretty little fangirls with pouty lips and perfect top knots.

But Talon ... he only wants a piece of me.

And four straight years of infuriating rejection means I'm almost positive he'd take a night with me over a national championship trophy. But I'm no fool—he only wants me because he can't have me. And with graduation approaching, time is running out. He's more desperate than ever, pulling out all the stops and doing everything in his power to get in my good graces.

They say, "Don't hate the player, hate the game."

But to that I say, "Why not both?"

I have my reasons ...

Sorry, BMOC. This victory? Not going to happen.

Take this shirt over these shoulders, throw it against the wall.
I want to hear the sound when it falls to the floor.
Take those wild hands and let them loose,
let them roam and find freedom where they wish.
I am here, right here, destroy me with passion.

—Tyler Knott Gregson

CHAPTER 1

Irie

"I HEARD he's a total dick. Is it weird that I'm turned on by that?" A freshman girl nibbles on the tip of her pen as she chats up her friend. Her long leg is crossed over the other, foot bouncing.

"Is it weird that you're turned on by that?" her friend spits her question back at her with a side of sass. "No. I saw the guys you hooked up with last fall. You have a type and that type is *shameless asshole*."

Amused, I fight a smirk and turn away, attempting to tune them out.

It wasn't all that long ago that I was in their position; a bright-eyed and bushy-tailed freshman surrounded by a plethora of hot co-eds. But I made the decision after the first month (and after being propositioned repeatedly by horny drunks and pursued by an impressively persistent quarterback with an oversized ... *ego*), that I'd remain focused on my studies.

Sure I've had a boyfriend or two along the way, but hooking up for the sake of hooking up isn't my style. But more power to the girls who can rock that walk of shame like no one's business, racoon eyes and sex hair and a satisfied flush on their rosy cheeks.

Yanking my pristine rose-gold notebook from my messenger bag, I flip to the first page before readying my favorite gel pen with the bronze-colored ink. Drowning in an ocean of open MacBook Airs with gleaming retina displays, I prefer to take notes the old-fashioned way. Swimming away from the current is kind of my thing.

I scan the room of baby-faced Pacific Valley University freshmen and check the clock. Three more minutes until class starts. Last semester, my advisor informed me I needed one more general elective to satisfy my graduation requirements and she gave me the choice between *Anthro 101* ... and *Philosophy of Logic*.

It was a no-brainer for me.

People have always fascinated me, especially when observed from a distance. And in this case, you can't get more distant than a couple hundred centuries or tens of thousands of years.

In the front of the lecture hall, a silver-haired professor in a kitschy Hawaiian shirt and wrinkled cargo shorts messes with a finicky projector, and to my left, two girls discuss weekend party plans as their overpowering perfumes compete for the oxygen I'm attempting to breathe.

Two rows up, a couple of scrawny guys are hitting on a lilac-haired wallflower who clearly wants nothing to do with them. She has my full sympathies, and I'd intervene if I were closer.

Oh, freshmen.

Out of nowhere a second later, a crumpled paper soars

through the air, landing at my feet. I kick it away before glancing over and spotting a couple of guys at the end of the row hiding their snickering faces.

Four more months and I'll be out of here forever.

"Holy shit," one of the girls beside me whispers, nudging her friend. "Isn't that Talon Gold?"

The other girl gasps, fanning herself and bouncing in her seat as she leans in and mumbles "dibs."

I'm midway through jotting today's date on the upper righthand corner of my paper when I glance up to find none other than Pacific Valley University's star quarterback and ladies' man extraordinaire climbing the steps two at a time ... making a beeline to the back row—to *my* row.

The girls beside me are giggling now, whispering about all the dirty things they want to do with him. The brunette on the left tightens and fluffs her top knot and the sandy blonde next to her casually dips her hand into her bag to retrieve a rollerball of pink lip gloss.

"Um, I'm sorry. Would you mind scooting down one spot?" The girl with the top knot leans across her friend's lap, tapping me on the knee.

"Oh my God, *Kaitlynnnn,* don't be rude," her friend scoffs at her before massaging her juicy-wet lips together. She turns to me. "Ignore her. She thinks she actually has a chance with *Talon Gold.*"

I want to tell them to stop acting like he's some demigod, to stop referring to him by his entire name like he's some iconic celebrity, because he's just a guy.

A mere mortal.

An arrogant asshole well aware of his disgustingly unfair good looks and propensity for scoring touchdowns—and hot chicks—in record-shattering numbers.

A man with zero shame and zero fucks to give.

Though I guess if the one girl prefers guys who are "dicks" it would make sense that she'd be fawning over this one.

Talon Gold is the King of Dicks.

"I can't believe this," Kaitlyn grabs her phone, firing off a text. "Monica is going to *freak* when I tell her he's in my class."

Her friend sits stunned and speechless as he gets closer. I don't even know that she's blinked since she spotted him.

"God, he's beautiful, isn't he?" Kaitlyn releases the dreamiest of sighs. "The bleached hair, the dark roots. I just want to run my hands through it, mess it up a little more. And that bronze skin. What do you think he tastes like?"

Southern California is practically a factory that mass produces guys exactly like him—the silver spooned, privileged kind whose multi-millionaire daddies write fat checks to the best athletic trainers in the world so their kids can become star college athletes and have all-you-can-eat buffets of college pussy while professors grade them on favorable curves so their report cards reflect the kind of grades they *should* be getting.

"Down girl," her friend says before swatting at her. "Okay, shut up now. He's almost here. Be cool."

I don't have to look up to feel his gaze pointed in my direction as he makes his way to the center of our row. A second later, he takes the lone empty chair next to mine.

"Irie, right?" Talon's long legs stretch wide, pushing into my space, his expensive sneaker stopping two inches from my knock-off Golden Goose sneakers.

Cute.

He's pretending like he *might not* know my name. He's pretending like he hasn't been trying to hook up with me since the fall semester of our freshmen year when I got roped into attending a party at some beer-scented three-story on frat house row and he cornered me the way a mountain lion corners prey, carefully stalking me first from all angles then making smooth and deliberate moves until he positions himself to go in for the kill.

Fortunately for me, his hunting skills were still in need of some fine-tuning back then.

I got away.

And I've gotten away every time since.

The auditorium hums with small talk. My body hums with electric amusement. Over the years, this has become a sort of game between us. Cat and mouse. Offense and defense. He's tried every strategy in the book, but I've managed to stick to the one that always works—cold, coy, aloof, and uninterested.

"All right, dudes and dudettes," the professor rests his hands on his hips, rocking back and forth on his heels as he scans the room. "I'm Dr. Longmire, but you can call me Rich if you want."

The girl to my left giggles to her friend. "He's not a *regular* professor, he's a *cool* professor."

"Welcome to Anthro 101." Dr. Longmire—Rich—twists the shark tooth necklace that hangs on a leather cord down his tanned chest as he paces the room. "We meet Mondays and Wednesdays from eight to nine with recitation on Fridays with my TA. You should have received your syllabus in your email over the weekend. If you need a paper copy, I've got a few on the desk up here. That said, I've been asked to remind you all that PVU is striving to become a paperless university. Please only print things when absolutely necessary."

One student gathers his things in a hurry and dashes out the side door. He's probably in the wrong classroom. It happens and it's no big deal, but it doesn't stop a group of meatheads in the corner from finding it hilarious and yelling out, "Loser!" just before the door swings shut.

Talon exhales, pinching the bridge of his nose.

Professor Longmire cracks a joke about how he doesn't usually scare people off until *after* he goes through his entire pitch.

No one laughs.

"You have a good winter break?" Talon asks me, leaning close and keeping his voice low. He's trying to feign intimacy, trying to act like we're more than the acquaintances we've only ever been. Smooth. But I see through it.

"The best," I lie, sparing him the details before pointing at the front of the room. "If you don't mind ..."

His heavy stare weighs on me, and a blanket of heat covers my skin in the seconds before the steady trot of my heart turns into an all-out gallop.

This happens every time—the ongoing war between my mind and body every time he comes around.

I'd be lying if I said his attention didn't flatter the hell out of me. I mean, come on. I'm only human—a mere mortal myself. I just happen to have a hell of a lot more self-control than the average SoCal blondie strutting PVU's seaside campus. I appreciate the attention, but by no means am I naïve enough to think there's anything special about it.

Talon wants to screw me.

And he only wants to screw me because he can't.

Nothing more, nothing less.

"Hey. You have a spare pen?" Talon asks with zero shame, his cinnamon-scented whisper tickling my eardrum.

Dipping down into my bag, I retrieve a hot pink gel pen—color choice unintentional—and hand it over without so much as making eye contact.

From my periphery, I watch as he examines it for a second before his full lips mouth a quick thank you. The garish color doesn't seem to faze him, doesn't so much as threaten his jock itch masculinity.

He flips to a clean page in his notebook—which is interesting since I've always taken him for a laptop kind of guy—and concentrates on the screen ahead.

"Now, I've been teaching here for over thirty years," Professor Longmire prattles on as he paces the front of the room. "I've been around long enough to know that these eight AM Monday classes are a pain in the you-know-what. I know not everyone is going to go to every single class. I know that there'll be times you're hung over or you oversleep or what have you. Don't email me. Don't send me your sob story or made up excuses. I don't want to hear it. Now some of the younger professors, they post lecture notes on the class website. But I don't have time for that. So here's what you're going to do. Everyone's going to have an accountability buddy."

"A what?" someone asks from the row before me.

"How old are we again?" one of the girls scoffs.

"I want you each to turn to someone next to you," he says. "That person is going to be your go-to when you need a copy of lecture notes. That person is also going to be your study partner. Their success is your success and vice-versa. Just because this is Anthro *101* doesn't mean it's an easy class. In fact, a quarter of you will drop out before the end of the semester, and the majority of you probably won't walk out of here with A's."

Two people—a guy and a girl from opposite ends of the room—gather their bags and show themselves out, heads tucked.

"*Aaaand* there we go. *That's* when I usually scare them

away." Longmire laughs at his own joke before scanning the audience. "Anyway, I'll give you all a moment to find your partner. Don't make a big deal of it, don't overthink it. Just pick someone—anyone—close by."

I gather a sea-salted lungful of air and take in my surroundings. The two girls beside me have suddenly replaced their disdain and are now clasping their hands together like a couple of junior high besties. The guys in the row ahead are already exchanging phone numbers, as are the guy and girl to their right. Within seconds, I surmise that everyone else around me seems to be spoken for—everyone, that is, except Talon.

Straightening my shoulders, I angle my body toward his and maintain a neutral expression.

The moment our eyes catch, he bites his lower lip and flashes a cockeyed smirk. "Guess it's us."

My stomach somersaults, but I play it cool. "Lucky me."

"Yeah." He laughs through his nose, his perfect white teeth flashing as he grins. "Lucky you."

CHAPTER 2

Talon

I'VE NEVER BEEN a believer in bullshit like fate or destiny, but after the way the stars aligned this morning, placing Irie Davenport not only in my sight but directly beside me—I'm willing to reconsider my stance.

"We should probably exchange numbers," I say to her as our anthro class is in the midst of a chaotic freshmen dismissal. "You know, since we're partners ..."

I refuse to use the word "study buddy."

It's just not sexy.

And partner has better ... *connotations*.

Irie flips to a page in the back of her little pink notebook and scribbles something before tearing the page, folding it into thirds, and handing it over. A second later, she slings her messenger bag over her lithe shoulder and tucks a strand of silky caramel-blonde hair behind one ear, revealing a simple golden stud. It's unpretentious and unexpected—much like her.

"Wait," I say after unfolding and scanning the paper. "This is your email."

"Yep." Her expression is bland and indifferent, and it's the same one she's been giving me for the last four years, but her violet eyes flicker with life. With all her years of practice, she's never been able to master the art of the true poker face. There's a part of her—however miniscule it might be—that wants me just as much as I want her.

I see it.

I fucking *feel* it.

And if I feel it, I know Irie does too.

I tend to be numb to most things, most of the time, but not this. Not her. Not us—or rather, what we could be.

Our tension has been ripe since day one, so palpable you could slice it clean with an obsidian knife. Why she tries to fight it and deny it is the one thing I've yet to figure out.

For years, I've been trying to get her number.

And for years, she's rebuffed me eight ways from Sunday.

"What if I need you right away?" I ask.

"Then you'll send me an email and it'll go straight to my phone," she says as she begins to navigate her way down the row.

Most girls love to be needed.

Not Irie.

I grab my shit and follow closely.

"What if *you* need *me*? I don't always check my email." It's the truth, but now that we're partners, I'm going to have to change that.

"I won't need you," she says when she reaches the end of our row. "I never miss a class."

Her hand, soft and delicate with glossy nails the color of

the sky, glides down the railing as she makes her way to the lower half of the auditorium. The faint scent of her wildflower perfume catches in her breeze and I steal a generous inhalation, though it hardly satisfies.

I want to smell it on her skin—warm and brilliant, alive.

I also want to run my hands along her curves and bury my face between her thighs and hear her soft voice in my ear as her limber body melts beneath mine.

I want her nails digging so hard into my backside they leave marks for days. Marks I'd earn. Marks I'd deserve …

I could make her feel so fucking good if she'd just let me.

One night.

That's all I want, all I *need* with Irie Davenport.

I want to unwind her, untighten that coiled personality. She's guarded and private, unlike the other girls who throw themselves at me and the second they're finished riding my cock, they lie in my arms and tell me their life stories like I give a shit. But Irie is different. She's not from around here—someone told me she's from the Midwest—and she's not an open book.

She's a padlocked diary.

A padlocked diary who wants nothing to do with me.

"Do you want my email just in case?" I ask, sounding like a schmuck as we pass through the door and into the hall. We're side by side now but seconds from losing one another in a sea of shoulder-to-shoulder students.

"If I need it, I'll look it up in the student directory," she says.

"Cool, cool. See you Wednesday," I say, but she's already disappeared into the crowd.

Rebuffed again.

It's not the first time.

And it sure as hell won't be the last.

But I walk away with a smile the size of Texas and the swell of hope in my chest—no different from the feeling I get when I lead the team onto the field during the opening game of the season.

In football, when you see an opening, you take it. You hold onto the ball with your life and you run like fucking hell until you score—or at least until you advance the ball.

I've been advancing the ball since the first time I laid eyes on Irie at Collin Holbrook's house party freshman year, and I've been running like hell ever since, but with four months until graduation, the end zone is finally in sight.

My cock swells in an anticipation of my sweetest victory yet.

I'm finishing the year with that touchdown.

CHAPTER 3

Irie

"AUNT BETTE, I'M HOME," I call as I hang my bag on the back of a kitchen chair. "Brought you dinner from the deli. Got that soup you like."

I place the brown paper bag on the counter and trek to the living room to find my great aunt passed out in her recliner while the TV in the corner plays Wheel of Fortune. Well, technically she's not *my* great aunt. She's my mother's brother's wife's aunt ... but in the grand scheme of things, it doesn't matter because she's cool as hell and I'm honored to be related to her in any capacity.

"Hey," I say softly, placing my hand on her shoulder until she stirs.

"Irie. Hi." She blinks a couple of times. "What time is it?"

I lower the footrest of her chair, fold her crocheted throw, and help her to the kitchen. At eighty-three and a hair under five feet tall she gets around well enough, but I still like to do anything I can to make her life that much easier.

Also, it's kind of why I'm here …

Four years ago, she offered to pay my college tuition and let me live with her for free—she only asked that I be her caretaker, which mostly consisted of running her errands, getting groceries, preparing basic meals, and maintaining the house inside and out. It was kind of strange at the time because I'd never met my mother's aunt before. She lived in Southern California and I grew up in middle-of-nowhere Missouri.

It was a lot to think about at first … committing to four years of living with and caring for a complete stranger.

But the first time we met, she offered eighteen-year-old me a fuzzy navel wine cooler and told me stories from her stint as a strip club manager in the seventies.

We've kind of been best friends ever since …

Aunt Bette's slowed down quite a bit over the last few years, though—particularly over this past winter break, when she spent nearly the entire month of December at the hospital battling a stubborn case of pneumonia. Every waking hour of Winter break was spent by her side, reading her the latest gossip articles from her favorite magazines, discussing her case with the doctor when necessary, sharpening her colored pencils and organizing her adult coloring books so she had something to do when she wasn't sleeping.

Fortunately Aunt Bette was more tenacious than the pneumonia, but things were looking dicey for a while.

"Your dinner's ready," I tell her as I lead her into the next room. "Fletcher's Deli. You're lucky. Got the last of the Irish potato soup."

I get her situated at the table before retrieving her soup

and turkey club. Normally I'd make her a quick dinner myself, but I lost track of time at the library tonight.

"How was your first day back?" she asks as I peel the plastic wrap from her disposable soup spoon. "What classes did you have?"

"Anthro, Hospitality Design, and Interior Lighting," I say. "And they were fine."

"Can't believe you're almost done." Aunt Bette smiles to cover the uncertainty in her eyes. "Seems like yesterday you were just starting."

She knows I can't stay here with her forever.

In four months, I'll be flying the coop.

And while I've loved our time together—especially since it's the first time in my life I've ever felt like I truly had a home—I can't stay here forever.

Last summer, I interned for a local designer named Kira Kepner. Just last month, she contacted me, saying she's been wanting to open a location up north in Malibu and she thinks I'd be the perfect designer to lead that team.

I almost choked when she gave me the salary.

I haven't told Aunt Bette yet, but I'm going to accept the offer.

Working for someone like Kira while I build my portfolio and having a cushy income to pay the bills is more than I ever could have dreamed for myself at this point. Most interior design grads start out at the bottom, clawing their way up to prove themselves, all the while dealing with juvenile drama and salty competition and making the kind of money that necessitates a part-time job and a couple of roommates to help pay the rent—at least in this part of the country.

California isn't cheap.

But now that I've lived here for almost four years, I can't

imagine living anywhere else, and I sure as hell have no plans to return home.

Missouri is great if you like farms and cornfields, if you're into the Chiefs and the Royals and the Cardinals, if you can't live without friendly folks with Midwestern manners, and if you gravitate toward the idea of living on the same street your whole life and raising a family of five with your high school sweetheart.

But those have never been my calling.

I've always wanted ... something else.

"Aren't you going to eat?" Aunt Bette asks.

"I had a granola bar on the bus," I tell her.

She rolls her eyes before tearing her sandwich in half, placing it on its waxy paper wrap, and sliding it to me. "I'll be damned if I sit here having a proper meal while you're wasting away on chocolate chips bars."

I take a bite, but only because I know she won't let it go. "Thank you."

I enjoy taking care of Aunt Bette, but sometimes I think she enjoys taking care of me more. She never married, never had kids. I'm the closest thing she's ever had to a daughter. In fact, not long after I moved in, she told me one night over bourbon-spiked coffee that she wished she would've known all those years ago what I was going through—both before living with Uncle Michael and Aunt Elizabeth ... and after.

She said she would have moved me out here sooner, would've taken me under her wing and given me a real home.

But it's okay.

She didn't know. She couldn't have known.

And at least we have now.

I finish the rest of my half of Aunt Bette's sandwich. "I

should head back, going to check my email and head to bed early."

She snorts. "Well, don't go to bed *too* early."

"As long as *you* don't stay up *too* late," I tease her back before disappearing down the hall.

As soon as I get to my room, I pull my laptop from my bag and connect it to the charger on my desk. I wait for the light to turn green before gathering my hair into a messy ponytail and heading to the bathroom to wash up for bed. When I come back, I change into a faded t-shirt and cotton pajama bottoms.

The shuffling of Aunt Bette's feet down the hall is followed by the sound of her laughter. She says something else, though I can't make out the words. She must be on the phone with one of her girlfriends. They always call each other around this time of night, and tomorrow is Bunko day at Sheila Carlisle's house.

I carry my laptop to the bed and climb under the covers, opting to check my email before calling it an early night.

Most students my age are living in campus town apartments, sitting around their kitchen islands shooting the shit with their bestie roommates over takeout pizza, putting their homework aside to catch up on the latest episode of The Bachelorette, helping each other decide whether to swipe left or right on the newest dating app.

While my college experience living off-campus has been less than typical, I wouldn't trade it for the world. I love living with Aunt Bette. She's my spirit animal.

And she's been better to me than anyone ever has—better than I probably deserve if I'm being honest.

I flip the lid of my laptop open and tap in my password. The screen flashes to life and I double-click on the PVU email icon on my desktop.

Five new emails.

I go through them, starting from the bottom. Most of them are campus-wide emails, reminders about deadlines and policies or upcoming events.

Delete, delete, delete ...

But it's the last one that catches me by surprise.

TO: davenport.irie@pvucampusmail.edu

FROM: gold.talon@pvucampusmail.edu

SUBJECT: Hey lucky ;)

MESSAGE: Just touching base ... if you ever need to get a hold of me, my number is 555-8851.

Unimpressed yet indubitably amused, I shut the lid, fling my covers aside, and return the computer to the charger.

Does he actually believe that knighting me with some stupid nickname and using a wink is the way to my heart? And my God, he must be so proud of himself for finally finding a way to get his number in my hands after all these years.

I roll my eyes when I return to my bed, the image of Talon high-fiving his football player buddies filling my mind. But that image is quickly replaced with other images —actual ones—of Talon over the years.

Talon at parties, surrounded by girls.

Talon's picture plastered on the front page of the PVU Daily during football season.

Talon on bus signs, the face of the PVU Tigers.

Talon eye-fucking me in passing by the campanile last fall ... it was so penetrating and intense I lost my train of thought as I was mid-conversation with a friend and almost tripped over a crack in the sidewalk.

Sliding under my covers, I close my eyes tight and

remember the cinnamon scent of his breath against my ear, the undeniable heaviness of his stare. I imagine what his hands—calloused and rough—might feel like in my hair, his thumb tracing my jaw as he claims my mouth like a man who's been starving for that very kiss his entire life, a man about to make a meal of me.

My stomach reels and my heart hitches and my skin is hot to the touch.

Every part of me comes alive when I think of Talon Gold.

The man is pure sex, power and dominance, and he could give me one hell of a night, I'm sure of it. But my guilty-pleasure reveries are as close as I'll ever get to letting him have his way with me.

Just as he has his reasons for wanting me, I have my reasons for not wanting him ...

... and my reasons are rooted deeper than he could possibly begin to understand.

CHAPTER 4

Talon

"IRIE, HEY." I rise from my seat in the back of the auditorium Wednesday morning, making a show of waving her down and getting her attention though we've yet to make eye contact.

Everyone around us stares—at me and at her. Some cruel. Some curious.

The heat is on. She can't keep acting like she doesn't see my little production.

"Irie, over here," I say, hands cupped around my mouth.

She finally glances up, gives the smallest of nods to acknowledge me, and then heads my way.

"Saved you a seat," I say when she gets closer. "Figured we should sit together again. You know, since we're partners or whatever."

I offer her a wink, like we have some kind of inside joke now, but I get crickets.

Irie lets her messenger bag slide off her shoulder before

taking the chair to my left. She smells cotton candy sweet with a touch of vanilla and her nails are painted a different color today—the palest of pink. The gold studs in her ears from the other day have also been replaced, this time with oversized tortoiseshell hoops.

I don't know why I notice these things about her. If it were any other girl, I couldn't care less. But with Irie, it's like I'm always trying to see what I can glean from all her little quirks and details.

Over the years, I've watched her style morph from semester to semester. I've watched her hair change from platinum to brunette to her natural caramel blonde and back. I've watched as she's drifted from one circle of friends to another—spending her time with economics nerds and English majors one year to the artsy-fartsy designer wannabes the next.

Sometimes I think she knows exactly who she is.

Other times I think she hasn't got a clue.

She might be surprised to know she isn't alone in that.

Some of us are just better at hiding it.

"You get my email?" I ask, referring to the one I sent on a whim Monday night. It was a desperate move and I fully own that, but after seeing her that morning, I couldn't get her out of my head the rest of the day. I couldn't stop thinking about what she smelled like and how her eyes almost smiled every time she looked at me even if her lips were not. I couldn't stop obsessing over seeing her again ... and I let my impatience get the best of me.

The instant I sent the damn thing I cringed—physically cringed.

I don't know what it is about her that throws me off my game every damn time.

And who the fuck uses terms like "touch base?"

"Yep," she says, hunched down as she retrieves her notebook and pen. Everyone else around us has their laptops out, prepped and ready to take notes when class starts in a few minutes, except us.

"Good deal." I tap my pen against my notebook, remembering I still have her hot pink one in my bag. I forgot to give it back last time but in my defense, she couldn't get out of here fast enough.

Professor Longmire flicks the lights off down in front, turning the auditorium dark except for the glow of the projector screen.

It makes me think of being at the movies, which then makes me think about the fact that I can't remember the last time I took a girl on an actual date. There was this one chick freshman year ... took her to dinner and a movie on Friday night ... and by the time Monday rolled around she'd all but broadcasted to the entire school that we were dating—as in boyfriend/girlfriend.

Twitter. Facebook. Instagram. Snapchat.

She made it as official as she possibly could, hashtagging the hell out of my name in every combination she could think of as well as posting a selfie she took of the two of us when I wasn't looking.

Fucking. Psycho.

I swore off dating after that and decided to focus solely on football with a side of academics.

A week later Irie Davenport walked into my life, and she's been dancing circles around my mind ever since.

Professor Longmire drones on about some ancient civilization down below. Irie scribbles notes as fast as she can, pausing every so often to chew on the cap of her pen. She looks so serious, so deep in thought, like she's in her own world.

I try to focus on the lecture, but sitting next to Irie is a constant distraction.

Every time she crosses and uncrosses her legs, every time she softly clears her throat or tucks her hair behind her ear, every time she so much as shifts, the world around me blurs into the background and my attention draws to her like a magnet no matter how hard I try to redirect it.

It also doesn't help that we're in the midst of an unseasonably warm January day and she's currently in nothing more than a strappy cotton tank and cut-off jean shorts that showcase her long, toned legs.

What I wouldn't give to have those legs wrapped around me ...

And they will be.

Eventually.

I steal another glance from the corner of my eye. Sweet Jesus, I don't even think she's wearing a bra. My palms flash hot as I imagine the feel of her creamy tits against them, and my cock strains against the inside of my jeans.

Longmire finishes his lecture after an hour, flicking on the main lights without any kind of warning. My eyes sting until they adjust and Irie gathers her belongings like she's got a plane to catch in some terminal in BFE.

"Oh, one more thing before you go," Longmire says. "Every Friday in recitation, there will be a ten-question quiz on the week's lessons. I *highly* suggest you study for these as half the questions are essay."

I glance at Irie, who doesn't seem the least bit fazed by any of this.

Quizzes have never been my strong suit. Shit, who am I kidding? Academics have never been my strong suit. But I'll be damned if I look like a C-average moron in front of my *partner*.

In front of *her*.

Following Irie toward the exit, I catch her before she disappears into the crowd like last time. "Hey, we should probably study for that quiz."

"I knew you were going to say that," she says as we walk together, her emotionless stare focused ahead.

"Tomorrow night," I say.

She's quiet at first, striding through the crowd to the building's exit, but I keep up with her, damn near shoulder to shoulder.

"All right," she says, exhaling. "When?"

"Six," I say.

Her lips press together. "Fine. We'll meet at the library."

I'm sure she assumed I was going to invite her to my place, but my loudmouthed roommates would ruin this careful song and dance we're in the midst of in two seconds flat by making some smart-ass comment.

I can't risk that.

We step into the daylight, sneakers soft against the sidewalk. People gawk at us walking together, and a couple of girls size her up with envious scoffs, though Irie doesn't seem to notice. Or if she does, she doesn't care.

"Cool. It's a date," I say.

Irie shoots me a look. "No, it's not."

Her full cherry lips wrestle the smallest hint of a smirk.

I give her a wink and then I head west to my next class.

I don't care what she says, it's a date.

And it's going to be the hottest fucking date she's ever had.

CHAPTER 5

Irie

HE'S EARLY.

I walk through the automatic doors at Belhaven Library and find Talon standing in the center of the atrium—hands deep on his pockets, head cocked, and eyes lit the second they steal mine.

"Study rooms are taken," he says. "But I found us a quiet corner on the third floor."

I tighten the grip on my bag. "Thanks."

He turns on the heels of his pristine sneakers and leads me to the stairs. "How was your Thursday?"

"Amazing," I say. If he knew me, he'd know how much I loathe small talk. But he doesn't know me so I won't hold it against him.

Surprisingly, he picks up at the sarcasm in my tone, chuckling under his breath as he glances back at me.

We climb another level of stairs and arrive at the third

floor, where he leads me to a cozy corner in the paleontology section.

"I'm getting some major *Land Before Time* vibes here," I say as I take a seat in an orange chair with scratchy, pilled fabric.

"Really? Because I was thinking more along the lines of Jurassic Park," he says, sitting beside me. "The original. Not the new ones. The new ones are shit."

I shrug. "I wouldn't know."

His jaw falls. "Wait. You haven't seen the new ones?"

"Nope."

"Then you should," he says.

"You literally just said they were 'shit' a few seconds ago," I say. I know where he's going with this. He's going to invite me over to watch them with him. "I'll pass."

"You didn't let me finish." He holds up a hand big enough to wrap around a football. "They're shit compared to the originals. But they're still decent. Jurassic Park movies are like pizza—even when they're bad, they're still good."

"Nice save, but I'm still going to pass." I check the time on my phone. "We should get started ..."

"Right." He grabs a notebook from his bag and flips it open to a page scribbled in hot pink ink—his notes from the first day of class. A moment later, he scoots his chair closer to mine, so close, in fact, that I can smell the hot, sweet cinnamon wafting from his mouth. "Where should we start? What it means to be human or the importance of evolution to anthropologists?"

"First one." I pull my notebook out, along with my tablet, and then I grab my textbook. "You read the first thirty pages, right?"

Talon's dark brows rise and he blows a breath between his full lips.

"You didn't do the required reading?" I ask.

"He never said anything about reading ..."

My brows knit and I tuck my chin. "Yes he did. The first day ..."

I'm not sure how he could have missed it. Longmire only brought up the reading assignment four separate times. Maybe if he wasn't so busy shamelessly staring at me from the corner of his eye ...

"You're going to want to read the first two chapters tonight," I say. "It's only thirty pages, but it goes a lot more in depth than the lectures did."

He scribbles a note to himself on his paper. "Chapters one and two. Got it."

I inhale another lungful of cinnamon, watching his steady hand glide the pen across his paper. He has great handwriting, especially for a guy. It's neat and straight and legible, all lower-case with extra kerning between the letters.

But I don't tell him that because it's irrelevant and I don't want him thinking I'm *that* easily impressed despite the fact that I've always been a details kind of girl.

"Why are you taking Anthro 101 anyway?" he asks.

"I needed another elective. You?"

"Retake," he says, lips pressed flat like he isn't proud of his answer. "Screwed around too much freshman year and had to take an incomplete."

A couple of girls with matching Lululemon leggings and messy topknots stroll past us, taking their time in hopes that Talon Gold might notice them, but he doesn't look away from me. Not once.

I'm sure if I weren't here, he'd be all over that. He'd be all smirks and eye-fucks and piling on the charm like there's no tomorrow.

I've seen it before. I've seen him in action too many times to count in all his BMOC glory.

This is nothing more than Talon Gold on his best behavior.

His fingertips graze the top of my knee, sending a kick-drum start to my heart.

"Did you hear what I said?" he asks. His touch abandons my skin, leaving an electric tingle in its place.

"No. Sorry. What?" I tuck a strand of hair behind my ear.

"I said we should read our notes and then quiz each other," he says.

How I missed that, I'm not sure, but I give him a nod. "All right."

Sinking back into my seat, I scan the words on the page, only by the time I get to the next set of bullet points, I can't remember any of what I've just read.

This never happens.

I don't lose my concentration this easily.

If anything, I'm normally too focused. I can make the outside world around me disappear with the mental snap of a finger. It's an old trick I picked up as a kid, when life got to be too much and I wanted to fade away. I couldn't fade away but I could ignore everything around me, and it was almost the same thing.

"You ready?" he asks after a few minutes. I'm not, but I nod anyway. "I'll quiz you first."

He leans across and gently tugs my notebook out of my hands, his mouth inching up at the sides until a flash of a dimple appears.

"What is anthropology?" he asks, sitting up straight and using a serious professor-like tone. He even pretends to shove imaginary glasses up the bridge of his nose. He's trying to be cute, trying to make me laugh.

And damn it.

It's working.

I fight a chuckle before clearing my throat. "The study of human societies and cultures over time."

"And what does it mean to be human?" he asks.

"That's a loaded question. Objective too. I don't think he's going to quiz us on that, do you?" I ask.

Talon shrugs. "Not sure, but I'm willing to bet you one shark tooth necklace that he will."

"Then I'll see your shark tooth necklace and raise you one Hawaiian shirt that he won't." My cheeks flush. I'm flirting back with him and I shouldn't be because I know better ... but he's sitting there all smiles and dimples and acting cheesy and giving me his full attention, and my weak little ego is lapping it up like a kitten to warm milk.

"Talon, hey." A baby-faced guy with dreads and a linebacker's build walks into our bubble out of nowhere, his arm outstretched for some kind of football player slash bro handshake. "What's up, man?"

"Trey," Talon says as he rises and gives him some kind of half-hug. "Not much, how you doing? You have a good break?"

"Yeah, yeah, man. Haven't seen you in the gym. You staying on top of everything?" his friend asks. "Don't let that arm go to shit all because the season's over. Heard you're being scouted pretty hard."

"Been working out at night," he says. "And yeah, I've had some offers."

"When you going to sign, man?" Trey asks. "You holding out for something? Dude, there are guys who would give their left nut for half of what you're probably being offered. You doing all right, man?"

I check my watch. I've only got another half hour before I have to leave to catch the bus.

"You know how it is. Fine print and hoops to jump through and all that," Talon says before giving his friend something I can only interpret as a goodbye handshake. "I'll keep you posted though when it happens. Good seeing you."

A moment later, the linebacker guy is on his way and Talon settles back into his seat.

"Sorry about that," he says.

I shrug like it's no big deal. And it isn't. I get it. Back in Missouri, the football players at my high school were gods—and not just demigods ... actual gods who wielded social power and ruled the school. And the quarterback? He was the god of the gods. Everyone looked up to him. The girls wanted to screw him and the guys wanted to be him. He couldn't go anywhere without being stopped and bothered—and there were even a few times when people would approach him and ask for his autograph or a selfie. It was usually kids or junior high pre-teens but to them, he was just as famous as Tom Brady. A local hero.

It was cute at first.

Until it wasn't.

Being the girlfriend of someone like that is the last thing on earth I ever plan to experience again—and I have my reasons.

"Okay, let's get back on track," I say. "Ask me something else."

Talon scans his notes. "Name three different types of anthropology."

Dragging in a stale breath of library-book scented air, I say, "Biological, social, and archaeology."

"Perfect," Talon says, his green eyes flicking to mine. I never realized how brilliant they were before—like a mix between emerald and turquoise.

An older woman in khakis and a PVU polo shuffles toward us, the frown on her face coming into focus. "I'm sorry, but this is a *silent* study area, not meant for chit chat. I'm getting noise complaints about the two of you over here. I'm going to have to ask that you find a study room or relocate yourself to the outdoor commons."

I begin to gather my things as Talon apologizes and the librarian disappears around the corner. I have no idea who could have complained as we've only seen a handful of people since we've been here, but whatever.

"You want to go to the commons?" he asks, referring to the wide-open greenspace outside the library. Most of the time there's where students play frisbee or hackysack or once in a while engage in LARP gatherings. It's almost always bustling and noisy and the worst kind of place to study for a test. Not to mention it's mid-January and brisk as hell. The idea of leaving the toasty library to sit outside and shiver for the next thirty minutes holds zero appeal.

"It's kind of chilly out," I say, squinting past him and out the floor-to-ceiling window.

Talon wastes no time digging into his backpack. A second later, he retrieves a zip-up hoodie the color of a grey SoCal sky in the wintertime.

"Here," he tosses it to me. "Wear that."

"What are you going to wear?"

"I'll be fine," he says, standing to gather his things.

I slip his hoodie over my shoulders, ignoring the fact that it stops just above my knees and is comically enormous on me. The faded scent of fabric softener and cologne envelops the air around me.

Talon watches me mess with the zipper and then he wears some half-cocked smirk as his stare lingers.

My stomach flips, but I don't allow myself to accept the compliment or read into the fact that he's looking at me the way a guy would look at some girl prancing around half-naked in nothing more than one of his old t-shirts.

"Ready?" he asks.

A couple of minutes later, we manage to find an unoccupied plot of grass in the back corner of the commons. It's getting darker with every passing moment, the sky transitioning from a peachy pink horizon to an ombre midnight blue directly above us—stars and all.

If this were a date—which it isn't—this would be the perfect backdrop.

I take a seat on the cold ground, the mild wintry wind kissing my face, and Talon cozies up beside me, so close his knee is almost touching mine. It's strange, but we've yet to reach for our notebooks. We just sit here, silent, eyes locked under a moonless sky.

A shiver runs through me, though I'm not cold.

I'm quite warm in his hoodie.

"*No freaking way,*" a girl's voice fills the space behind us. I turn and spot Kaitlyn from Anthro gawking at us. She can't grab her phone fast enough and within seconds she's tapping out a text to a mystery recipient.

Talon follows my gaze and then rolls his eyes. "Ignore her."

Without saying a word, I turn away and dust my palms together. Done and done.

I've been the target of many-a-mean-girl before. I'm practically an old pro at this.

A moment later, Kaitlyn is still standing a couple of yards behind us. "Becca, you're not going to believe this. Remember that girl from Anthro? She's studying with Talon outside the library right now. I know? I can't believe it either. Maybe there's hope for me after all."

Before I have a chance to process what she's just said, Talon's climbing up from the ground and marching over to the smart-mouthed little freshman.

"You mind?" he asks, hands on his hips. His brows are knit and his mouth is pressed flat. "Trying to study over here. And for the record, this?" He points his finger between the two of them. "Never going to happen. Lose the hope. There is none for you."

The girl's mouth is agape and her eyes are shiny as glass in the seconds before thick tears drip down her cheeks. Muttering into her phone, she ends the call, slides it into her bag, and stalks off.

"Little harsh, don't you think?" I ask when he returns.

"I don't tolerate that kind of shit. People who think they're better than other people for whatever asinine reasons their pea-sized brains cook up."

I'm speechless for a moment. Intrigued. Also impressed.

"You know we have to see her in class three days a week, right?" I ask. "She sat next to me the first day."

"If she's smart, she'll find a new place to sit. If she's not, well, it's going to be awkward for her but not me. And it shouldn't be for you either."

I lift my palms in the air. "It won't be. I just ... wow. I can't believe you did that."

"Want me to quiz you first?" he asks, switching gears.

He's over it. I am too. I don't like to give those kinds of people my time or energy if I can help it. Once upon a time,

I'd have let it ruin my day, my week, whatever. But time and distance have fixed my former weaknesses.

"Sure."

Talon retrieves our notebooks from his bag and hands them over. "Quick question, though, before we start."

"Okay ..."

"What are you doing tomorrow night?"

Just when I was beginning to think that he wasn't all that bad, that I could tolerate him for the rest of the semester, he goes and pulls *this*.

Was that an act earlier? Some kind of stunt he pulled to make me think he was a decent human being under all that ego? Real or fake, one thing's for sure: he's still a man on a mission.

And old mission.

One he's never abandoned no matter how futile the journey has gotten.

Without hesitation, I shove my things into my bag, unzip the hoodie, and hand it back. The cool air blankets my skin but I don't feel a thing.

"What?" he asks.

I try to speak again, but I'm at a loss for words.

"I'm *really* going to need you to accept the fact that I'm not going to date you," I say. "I'm sorry, but you're not my type. I don't know how else to make that clear to you. In fact, you're my anti-type."

"Is that even a thing?" He rises from the ground, his height forming a tower that cocoons the two of us.

"My point is," I say, arms crossed, "you have to stop asking me out. My answer's never going to change."

"One date," the relentless son of a bitch has the nerve to say. "One date and you'll never have to see me again."

"Look, I appreciate that you like a good challenge and

you like to win and all that, but this victory isn't going to happen for you, so maybe refocus your sights on someone else?"

His expression twists. "Someone else?"

"I could close my eyes and point to any girl walking past us right now and I'm one-hundred percent sure you could ask her out and she'd say yes," I tell him. "Win-win for both of you."

"*Someone else?*" he repeats harder, as though my suggestion disgusts him. "Irie, there *is* no one else. There's only you. There's only ever been you."

His words are a balm to the hammering chaos happening inside me right now—my heart has gone off its rails, my stomach is two seconds from upheaving itself, and my mind is thinking all sorts of thoughts that contradict and make zero sense ... and then he goes and says something like that.

There's only you. There's only ever been you.

I dated someone just like him once upon a time.

Dashingly handsome. Charismatic. Mr. Popular. Made me feel like it was just the two of us no matter where we were or how many people were around. Said all the right things. Did all the right things. Made the kind of promises a person could believe with every fiber of their soul.

I loved him harder than I'd ever loved anyone or anything in my life, with an intensity so dialed up it was as magical as it was terrifying.

But I was younger then. Too young to understand how something so beautiful could turn so ugly in the blink of an eye.

That boy might be long gone.

But the scars are permanent, everlasting.

And when I see Talon, I can't help but see the guy who came before him as they're cut from the very same cloth.

When I make a mistake, I never repeat it. Ever.

"Do me a favor and don't say stuff like that again, okay?" Slinging my bag over my shoulder, I head for the sidewalk that leads to the bus stop. "Bye, Talon."

"Irie," he calls after me.

But I don't stop.

CHAPTER 6

Talon

I STARE across the classroom Friday morning, restless and unsettled as my knee bounces. Irie showed up a minute late to recitation and took a seat at a table in the front—never mind the fact that there were three empty chairs at mine.

My eyes scan over the words on the test before me, but nothing makes sense.

I stayed up until almost one in the morning last night studying on my own and reading those two chapters in the textbook, but concentration came at a premium. I couldn't stop thinking about Irie. I couldn't stop replaying our time together at the library.

Everything was going well. I was making her laugh. Getting her to flirt back with me for the first time ever ...

I even gave her my favorite hoodie when we went outside because it was either that or call it a night, and I was just getting her warmed up.

But of course, the second I asked her out, it was game over.

I don't even think it's fair to say I advanced the ball.

My sexy enigma turned into this woman with cloudy eyes and crossed arms and an edge in her voice that wasn't there before.

Over the years, any time I'd ask her out, she'd give me a polite yet casual "no thanks" or come up with another way to gently let me down. But last night brought out a side of her I've never seen before.

I called out for her as she stalked off, but she ignored me.

And so I let her go.

Figured I was the last person she wanted chasing after her, especially since it was me she was running away from.

"If you're finished with your quizzes, bring them up here." A dark-haired TA in acid-wash jeans and a white Guns-n-Roses t-shirt is perched on the edge of a metal desk in front of a white board. Tattoos cover her fingers and the underside of her left forearm, and a silver hoop protrudes from her septum. She looks like she doesn't give a fuck about a damn thing (besides anthropology, I guess).

I blaze through the multiple-choice questions as fast as I can. I've always read it's best to go with your gut instinct on those rather than re-read and second guess and talk yourself out of your original answers.

I move onto the essay questions next, which are easier than I anticipated, most of them requiring nothing more than a few sentences at most.

When I get to the last one, I laugh to myself. Irie was right. Longmire didn't ask us about what it means to be a human. He probably didn't want to read through a hundred-plus psychobabble bullshit answers, and I don't blame him. I'm sure he'd much rather be catching waves.

Irie is one of the first to turn in her quiz. I scribble my final sentence and make my way to the front of the room, passing her table. She doesn't notice me. Or she pretends not to.

As soon as the final quiz has been submitted, the TA rehashes the week's lessons and dives deeper into biological anthropology, which conveniently happens to be her focus of study. My attention waxes and wanes and veers toward Irie. Or, rather, the back of her head—her shiny, glossy strands ironed straight and curtaining down to the middle of her back. She's facing forward, jotting down notes in her rose gold notebook while everyone around her is clacking away on MacBook keyboards.

My phone buzzes in my pocket, not once or twice, but three times, and I slide it halfway out to check my texts.

There's a party Saturday night.

At the Westbrook house—the twelve-bedroom three-story on Villanueva full of frat boy rejects—guys who partied too hard to stay in their fraternity's good graces.

Apparently my presence has been requested.

And requested.

And requested ...

Exhaling, I slide my phone back and ignore the series of vibrations that follow.

"Okay. I'm going to let you guys out a little early today," the TA says. Within milliseconds the group collects their things in one giant tandem effort.

Fucking freshmen.

Irie takes her time though. Shockingly, she doesn't have a plane to catch this time. I wonder if she's done with classes for the day—like me. In a perfect world, we'd be shooting the shit together all afternoon—preferably between the sheets ... or on the kitchen counter ... or in the back of an empty classroom if we're feeling particularly frisky.

Someday.

Someday soon ...

Rising, I shift my bag over my shoulder and head to her table, but she's oblivious as she heads out.

I manage to catch up to her halfway down the hall.

"Irie, wait up," I place my hand on her shoulder to stop her.

She spins around, peering up at me through a fringe of dark lashes. "Hi."

I want to ask her about last night—make sure we're still cool. But before I get a chance to say anything, I'm shoulder-checked by Vin Chalmers, a second-string running back who legitimately believes he's God's gift to football.

Some people fake it 'til they make it.

And some of us don't have to.

"Tal, you going to Westbrook Saturday?" he asks, lifting his meaty hand to give me a low five. "It's going to be lit. A bunch of A-Chi-O girls are going to be there."

He traces his tongue along his square teeth and flashes a confident grin in an unnatural shade of ice-white.

I turn to Irie—or where she *was*—and find an empty space.

A void.

Peering across the packed hallway, I find her already yards away, completely out of reach in every way.

"So you in or not?" he asks.

Westbrook parties are notoriously and historically epic. Would I rather be spending my Saturday night showing Irie Davenport the time of her life? Of-fucking-course I would.

But seeing as how that's not an option yet, I don't see any harm in having myself a good time.

"Yeah, man," I say. "I'm in."

"Oh my *gawd*, Talon Gold!" A girl with comically huge everything—tits, teeth, ass—trots toward me, her bony arms extended. "I haven't seen you *foreverrrr*! How the hell are you?"

She wraps me in a strawberry-mint scented embrace and squeezes me like a life preserver in a typhoon, bouncing and rubbing her body against every part of me.

Fuck if I can remember her name.

Pretty sure she blew me in a bathroom at a house party sophomore year, but that was lightyears ago. If I recall correctly, she threw a fit when I wouldn't fuck her so I slid my hands up her mini skirt, shoved her panties to the side, and fingered her until she came.

Twice.

"You going to the Westbrook party this weekend?" she asks as she releases her hold on me, blinking her oversized lashes, which I'm pretty sure are just as fake as the rest of her.

"Of course he is," Vin interjects. He studies my lackluster expression with a mix of curiosity and intrigue, though he doesn't bring it up.

"Awesome." She grins even bigger, her Chiclet veneers blinding and distractingly white. "I'll see you there."

As soon as she's out of earshot, Vin shakes his head. "You lucky son of a bitch."

"What?"

"You're *so* gonna hit that this weekend."

I scoff. "Nah."

"You don't want that?" he asks, eyes wild.

"Nope."

Vin cocks his head to the side, shooting me a look like I'm some kind of crazy bastard. "Fine. You don't want her, I'd be happy to take that off your hands."

"All yours."

"All right, man. Imma cut you loose," he says, walking backwards and pointing at me with finger pistols. "See you Saturday."

I give him a nod and head out, not giving the party another thought the second I hit the sidewalk. I'll go. I'll make an appearance, have myself a decent time, and give the people what they want—stories, pictures, and photo ops.

But come Monday, it's back on.

CHAPTER 7

Irie

I'M on my third Corona and fully feeling it. Pretty sure my blood is ninety-eight percent hops and barley at this point, but whatever. It feels good to be in the moment and not feel anything but the Velcro stickiness of my shoes against dirty floors.

"What are you doing?" My best friend, Brynn, stumbles into the kitchen of this godforsaken party house we're in Saturday night.

House parties have never been my thing.

I'm more of a chill-in-the-corner-of-a-hip-lounge-and-sip-cocktails kind of girl, but some guy Brynn's been pining after since spring semester last year invited her and she wanted a wingman, and so here I am.

"Are you ... *redecorating*?" Brynn stands back, slack-jawed and gawking.

"Organizing," I say, admiring my work. "Things are

more pleasing to the eye when they're grouped by item type and color."

I gaze along the messy counter which houses dozens if not hundreds of beer cans, wine bottles, and White Claws, all of them neatly sorted by flavor and color, their labels facing front like pint-sized soldiers.

"Now I'm going to rearrange their cutlery drawer because I don't know how the hell they find anything in—" I begin to say until Brynn grabs my hand.

"Irie," she says, head tucked down and eyes unfocused. She's far more drunk than me, but it doesn't stop her from attempting to be my voice of reason. "We're here to have a good time and there are twelve bachelors who live here. You think they give a shit if they can't find a butter knife?"

"*You're* here to have a good time," I remind her. "I'm just ... here."

"Stop being a wet blanket."

"That's not fair."

I love Brynn, but I resent any opinions that suggest in order to have a good time you have to be a cloned sheep in a massive herd.

She shrugs before bracing herself against me. "I'm sorry, but you're being a total lame ass right now. In all the years I've known you, I've only seen you let loose twice. Twice, Irie! And you know what? I freakin' love you to death, but that other girl was pretty dope and she deserves to come out and play ... especially tonight."

"What's so special about tonight?"

"Um, the entire PVU football team is here for one," she says.

My stomach drops, no ... plummets.

"You didn't tell me they were coming," I say.

In a flash of a second, I'm suddenly feeling extremely sober.

She laughs. "Why would I? You hate football. I didn't think you'd care."

Fair point.

I love Brynn and she's my best friend in the entire world, but she's also a diehard PVU Tigers fan and nothing in the world could change her mind. Her parents went to PVU. Her grandparents went to PVU. Her older brothers too. They're the most fanatical family I've ever known—they could even put some of the families back home in Missouri to shame with their extensive collection of fan gear.

A group of burly, muscled guys enter the kitchen one after another and I hold my breath, waiting for one of them to be Talon. I exhale when I scan their faces and don't find his.

"Hey, guys," Brynn says, tossing her raven waves over her left shoulder before settling behind the kitchen island and designating herself bartender. "What are we drinking tonight?"

The men—whom I recognize as Tigers—call out their orders and like a seasoned natural, she hands out drinks—and flirts. The guys seem to enjoy it enough, though I suppose it gets old after a while ... always having girls throw themselves at you, having people notice you everywhere you go.

They leave the room, drinks in hand, and Brynn is all smiles as she mouths, *"OH MY GOD."*

Pretty sure they just made her entire college career just now.

"Where's Nick?" I ask her. "The guy who invited you?"

She checks her watch, tapping through some text

messages. "Oh. He just texted me and said he's here. Somewhere. I should go find him."

"Yeah. You should." I wink at her before returning to my pet project. "Since that's why we came."

Organizing the cutlery drawer takes all of four minutes, and once I'm finished, I exhale, take a generous sip of my drink, and lean back against the island counter. The room around me sways. Or maybe I'm swaying. It's all the same at this point.

Pulsing and pounding music from another room rattles the window above the kitchen sink, and when I glance up, I fully expect to see my reflection staring back at me—only it isn't me.

Gasping, I grip the counter's edge and spin on my heels, coming almost face-to-face with none other than Talon.

His full mouth curls at one end. "Didn't mean to scare you."

Composing myself, I reach for my drink and stand back as he scans the array of beverages I've recently organized.

"You do this?" he asks, pointing.

"Maybe."

Talon smirks before selecting a Corona. He twists the cap and tosses it in an open-topped garbage can nearby. "Have to admit, kind of surprised to see you here. This doesn't seem like your kind of scene."

"It isn't." I shrug one shoulder before taking a sip.

"Then why are you here?"

I don't see how that's any of his business, but since he asked ...

"For a friend," I say. "She asked me to come."

"And then she ditched you?"

"I'm perfectly capable of walking into a party and finding something to do on my own."

He scratches at his temple. "It's just that most girls travel in pairs or packs or whatever."

"I'm not most girls."

"I know," he says without hesitation.

There's a vibration rattling in my chest, and it takes me a second to realize someone simply turned the music up.

Talon keeps his gaze trained on me and while he's distanced himself a few feet away, the walls around us continue to close in.

Heat prickles at my hairline and my skin flashes hot. With my stomach in knots, I drop my drink on the counter and make a beeline for the back door in desperate search for air.

The metal door slams behind me and I find myself on a small wooden deck with rotted floorboards and party lights hanging from above. Empty and over-turned red plastic cups litter the area around me and if I were feeling better, I'd stack them up and throw them away.

I can't stand a mess. I can't stand disorganization or chaos.

They say a frenzied childhood will do that to a person.

I take a seat on one of the steps leading to the back yard and rest my elbows on my knees.

Deep breaths ...

The creak of the door demands my attention a second later, and I turn back to find Talon standing in the doorway, his expansive frame blocking the light from the inside of the house and framing him in an ethereal glow at the same time.

"You okay?" he asks.

"Just needed some fresh air," I say. The night air is verging on bone-chilling, at least by SoCal standards, and I'm not sure how long I'll last out here, but I'm quite certain if I hadn't left the kitchen, I'd be standing in a pool of my own vomit right now.

"Mind if I have a seat?" he asks.

"Are you usually this polite when no one's looking?" I ask, scooting over.

"What do you mean?" He takes the spot beside me. The steps are narrow, maybe three or four feet wide if I had to guess, and our outer thighs are pressed against one another.

I rest my head against my hand, turning to look at him. "You have a reputation. And it isn't a nice one."

He laughs though his nose. "What have you heard?"

"That you're a dick," I say, recalling the time I watched him body slam another guy outside the Econ building. It was the Monday after a devastating Tiger loss and the guy was talking shit to Talon about some fumbled catch. "And I've seen you in action, so don't chalk it up to rumors."

"I'm only a dick when I have to be."

"No one *has* to be a dick."

"Maybe in your world." He glances into the yard, which is long and deep and turns into a pitch-black void halfway back.

"Please." I roll my eyes. If the man only knew what my *world* was like and how many times I'd have loved to be a dick to people ...

A guy and girl emerge from behind a tree in the dark distance. He zips his fly. She wipes her mouth on the side of her hand. They stumble off, disappearing around the side of the house hand in hand.

Ah, young love ...

I heard a girl talking once a few years back. She claimed she blew Talon at a party and as soon as he got his, he pushed her off him and refused to so much acknowledge her the rest of the night.

Maybe he felt the need to shoulder check the asshole talking shit about him after a bad game, but there's no excuse for being cruel to a girl whose only crime was worshipping his cock.

The door behind us swings open and slams shut, and the weight of heavy footsteps reverberates across the worn decking.

"Talon, there you are, man," a guy's voice says.

I don't turn around, I stare into the dark void ahead.

"Been looking all over for you," he adds. "You wanna come in? The A-Chi-O girls are here and we're about to do some body shots. Got a sexy redhead in there with your name on her. Don't keep her waiting."

Talon is hesitant at first, but he remains planted beside me. "Nah, man. I'm taking it easy tonight."

I give him a slow side glance.

"What? No way. You sure?" his buddy asks.

Talon waves him away. "Yep, I'm good. I'll catch you in a bit though."

His friend leaves and once again it's just the two of us.

"I hope you didn't do that for my sake," I tell him.

"You really think I'd rather be in there sucking Patron from some freshman's belly button than sitting out here with you? Under the stars?"

"Duh."

He brushes his shoulder against mine. "You're out of your mind, Irie Davenport."

No one ever calls me by my full name and in general, I find it a bit strange, but for some reason, coming from his lips with his crushed velvet voice vibrating in my ear, it sends my stomach into a somersault.

Silence settles between us, but in my defense, I don't know how to transition from that. He's pouring on the charm, trying so damn hard to get in my good graces, and I'd be lying to myself if I said I didn't enjoy it—at least a little bit.

Half of me wants to send him inside to the waiting human shot glass sorority chick.

The other half of me wants to linger in this moment, under the stars, beside the warmth that radiates off his body and onto mine.

"You know this house used to belong to the mayor," he says. "Like back in the nineteen twenties when this town was founded. It served as city hall for a while, when the first one burned down. And during the Vietnam War, it was a sort of halfway house for returning soldiers. In the eighties, I heard it was a brothel or something."

I shoot him a look. "Random."

"Thought you were into houses and all that," he says. "With your interior design major."

He isn't wrong.

"How did you know all of that?" I ask. "About the history of the house? Did you Google it when I wasn't looking?"

"My stepdad owns the place," he says. "He bought it back in the nineties when it was at auction. Fixed it up enough to turn it into a place he could rent to college kids. My mom wanted to do a full restore, make it look just like it did when it was first built. She's kind of an interior design junkie herself. But Mark wouldn't have it. He wanted to make a quick buck because that's what he does."

"Your family owns this house?"

"My stepdad does. Yeah."

"Why don't you live here?" I ask.

"You saw the current state of the inside, right? Would *you* live here?"

"No."

"I rest my case," he says.

"Doesn't your stepdad care that this beautiful house is being completely destroyed?"

"As long as it's padding his bank account, he couldn't give a shit less." He glances up at one of the lit windows on the second floor. The shadows of two people behind the sheer curtain leave very little to the imagination.

The last time I hooked up with anyone was almost a year ago, when I briefly dated this theater major who unironically turned out to be a bit too dramatic for my liking in the end. I'd never seen a man cry so much over *everything*. Sex with him was slow and meticulous, and I swear he tried to make it look the way it does in film and on television—like softcore porn. But it got to the point where it was distracting, and sometimes all I wanted was to fuck and to be fucked.

But those slow and sensual Oscar-worthy kisses ...

I miss the hell out of those.

"So your mom is into interior design?" I ask, trying to keep the conversation neutral and non-sexual in any way possible.

"Yeah, she actually used to have her own design firm," he says. "Back before she met Mark anyway. He's a builder and real estate developer and after they got married, she closed her freelance firm and worked with him on all his projects."

"Nice," I say.

"I swear every time I go home the house looks different. Hell, she even changes up my bedroom at least once a year."

I shrug. "I get it. Sometimes it gets old looking at the same things all the time. It's fun to switch things up."

"Yeah, but my room?"

"Maybe it reminds her of something she doesn't want to be reminded of?"

"Such as?" he asks.

"I don't know ... maybe when she looks at it, she thinks about her baby boy who's all grown up and maybe that makes her sad?"

Talon chuffs through his nose. "Pretty sure my mom hasn't felt a damn thing in at least fifteen years. Woman's got a whole cabinet full of shit that helps her not be sad."

He's quiet for a second, contemplative almost.

And then the door behind us creaks open.

The footsteps that follow are lighter. I don't have to turn around to know it isn't one of his linebacker buddies this time.

"Talon? Oh my God! Hey," a girl says. He turns to face her. I stare ahead as her over-the-top energy invades the crisp night air. "Coley said I'd find you out here. You should come in and do a shot with me for old times' sake!"

From my periphery, I see her manicured hand curl around his rounded shoulder as she crouches down.

The silence between the two of them is cringeworthy—at least for her—and I can almost feel her flittering glittery mood fading in real time.

"Y ... your friend can come too?" she offers, voice broken and confidence dashed.

"I'm good," I say, keeping my attention on the blackness ahead.

"Yeah, I'm good too," Talon says.

"You sure?" the girl asks.

The weight of Talon's attention blankets me. "Positive."

Without saying another word the girl traipses inside, her heels clunking across the wobbly deck boards. The door creaks open and slams a second later. I almost feel sorry for her.

Almost.

"You didn't have to do that for me," I tell him.

He scoffs, taking a sip of his beer.

"These are your glory days," I add. "You should enjoy them. Take full advantage. You shouldn't be pretending to be annoyed by all this attention all because you're trying to impress some girl who doesn't even want to be impressed."

"Not trying to impress you."

"Bullshit," I say, laughing. "You're a liar."

"All right." He nudges his shoulder against mine. "Maybe I am. Just a little."

"Well it ends here, tonight," I say.

"Just like that?" he asks. "And just because you say it does?"

"Pretty much." I stand, stretching my legs. A small shiver works its way through me and from here, the house looks warm and glowing and a million times more inviting than it did before.

Talon rises, towering over me with his eyes locked on mine. "Why do you hate me, Irie?"

"Just because you're not my type and I don't want to date you doesn't mean that I hate you, Talon. I don't even know you—how can I hate someone I don't know?"

"How do you know I'm not your type if you won't take the time to get to know me?" he asks.

Fair enough. "Maybe I don't know you, but I know enough about you to know you're not my type."

"Fuck types."

"Says the guy who's fucked half the school." I fold my arms and glance down. That was a little harsh even if it's true.

"That's what you think?" he asks.

I challenge myself to meet his accusatory stare, to own my stance. "I told you earlier ... you have a reputation. I've heard girls talk about hooking up with you. I've heard about the way you treat anyone who so much as thinks they might have a chance with you. Forgive me if I'm trying to steer clear of your warpath."

"Irie, *you are* the reason for that warpath," he says, his tone callous and his jaw flexing.

"So I'm supposed to be flattered? You treat other girls like crap because they're not me? Is that what you're trying to say?"

"You're oversimplifying."

"Am I though?" I angle my head to the side, my mouth twisted as I fight a smirk. Maybe I'm flirting. Maybe I'm also making a point.

Talon is looking at me like he's two seconds from devouring me—my mouth specifically. His tongue wets his full lips and his left hand tightens at his sides, like he has to refrain from allowing himself to touch me.

There's a lot of clout standing before me.

An insane amount of restraint.

He's mere inches from the only thing he wants—the only conquest he can't have—and it's physically torturing him.

To wield this kind of control over someone so powerful is a sensation unlike any I've experienced before ... and in an unexpected turn of events, my nipples harden, my sex tingles, and my lips swell with a curious ache.

In my defense, I'm not normally aroused by torturing people.

In his defense, he's not normally used to reoccurring rejection.

This is quite the standoff we have going.

"Where are you going?" he asks.

I look him up and down. "In."

"You cold?"

He's standing here in a gray V-neck t-shirt and ripped jeans. He has nothing to offer me but his arms and as cold as it is tonight, it's tempting.

But I won't let it get to that.

I climb the top stair step and make my way across the deck, walking backwards as my hands clasp. "Go have fun, Talon. It's a Saturday night. Do some body shots. Find a pretty little sorority girl and give her a night to remember. You're wasting your time with me."

I head back into the house before he has a chance to speak. Once in, I take a White Claw from the now semi-organized kitchen counter and follow the music, disappearing into some room with a sound system so loud it drowns out every last thought in my head—which is a good thing.

Because all of my thoughts?

They're about him.

CHAPTER 8

Talon

I LEAN against the wooden railing of the deck, watching the party house swallow Irie up as she heads in. Exhaling, my breath turns to clouds. No wonder no one's outside tonight. It's cold as fuck. Sitting next to her for the past twenty minutes, I've been so transfixed I haven't given the temperature a second thought.

The music pumps from inside, the pulsing baseline of some Avicii song rattling the windows every four seconds. I'm going to have to head in. I'm going to have to slap on a shitfaced grin, pretend there's nowhere else I'd rather be, and act like I'm not searching for Irie every time a pretty girl struts by.

Scraping my ego off the floor, I make my way inside, which now feels like a goddamned sauna. There are easily twice as many drunk bastards as there was before and it's so fucking loud I can't hear myself think—which is probably a good thing.

I grab a can of Miller Lite from the fridge since the ones on the counter are lukewarm. God forbid one of these pricks spends Daddy's money on a bag of ice to turn the sink into a cooler trough.

Amateurs.

Pulling the tab, I lift the can to my mouth and finish the beer in three swigs before deciding to follow it up with another.

"Whoa, dude, take it easy." Vin appears out of nowhere, slapping my back with a thick palm. "The night is young, my friend."

"No shit, moron. Gotta get this party started." I chug the second beer like a fucking man on a mission before grabbing a third—though this one will be more of a prop. I don't want to get sloppy drunk because that's a rookie move and no one ever looks good falling down and knocking into people. Besides, the last thing I need are four-hundred eighty-eight pics of myself shitfaced all over social media.

I've got a reputation to uphold.

Vin chuckles before plucking a room-temperature Corona from the counter. A second later, a pack of collar-popped guys come in, cases of Busch Light on their shoulders.

I get the hell out of there and head to the front room—a gargantuan space that once served as the mayor's formal receiving room, complete with a hand-carved fireplace surround and wooden marble mantel. My mother refused to let my stepfather tear out anything original to the house. I think she still dreams of fixing it up someday, but the Westcott house is situated along Tiger Way ... nestled between frat houses, sorority McMansions, and college bus stops. No one under the age of twenty-three is ever going to want anything to do with this house.

I find an empty section on a sunken plaid sofa by the window and take a seat. It takes all of three seconds for people to flock toward me. Some make it obvious. Some not so much.

"Hi." A pretty brunette with lips the color of ox blood perches on the arm beside me. "You're Talon, right?"

I recognize her now.

A cheerleader.

In high school, I chased every little short-skirted ponytail who so much as glanced in my direction. In college, the cheerleaders were notorious for fucking their way through the entire team, first string to second, running back to lineman.

"Bro, there you are." Vin ambles toward us, his thick mitts filled with tequila in mismatched shot glasses. A curly-haired blonde is behind him, a bowl of lime wedges and salt shaker in hand.

They clear a small section of coffee table in front of me and start handing out liquor and limes.

"Saved the biggest one for you, man." Vin hands me the tallest shot glass.

I force a smile before accepting it. The girl hands me a lime and then reaches for my arm, turning my wrist before bending to give it a lick, slow and seductive.

I jerk it away before her tongue contacts my flesh. "Nah, I'm good."

She recoils, her smile fading like I've burst some fantasy bubble of hers, and I toss the tequila back in one go, no chaser, letting myself feel the burn as it glides down my throat.

A group of girls walk past the room, making their way to the stairs. I glance up, searching for Irie. But of course she's not amongst them, and I should have known.

She's never been a pack animal.

"Talon, mind if I get a pic?" A girl with tits up to her chin squeezes behind the sofa, her phone camera readied as she positions herself behind me. "Smile!"

I do my thing as she snaps not one, not two, but five fucking pictures, and then she skips away like a giddy kid who just met Mickey Mouse at Disneyland.

My body sinks into the worn sofa, deeper, harder, heavier, as the alcohol hits my blood. I'm warm and numb and completely convinced I can suffer through the rest of his evening ... until I spot a guy and a sandy-haired girl on the other side of the room essentially fucking with their clothes on in a leather wingback chair.

For five solid seconds, I see Irie. I see a horny bastard with his hands on her ass. I see a jackass tasting the lips that should only belong to me. And I see her curved hips grinding against a dude that will never be able to satisfy her the way I could.

Then I see black.

With my jaw clenched, I rise from my spot and storm across the room.

They're oblivious to me ...

... until I grab his arm and all but yank him out of the chair.

"The fuck is your problem, man?" he asks, wild-eyed.

Irie scrambles off his lap—and it's then that I realize it isn't Irie.

It isn't Irie at all.

Just some girl with the same hair.

She covers her swollen lips with her hand and cowers in the corner as her boyfriend gives me a non-verbal what-for. His hands are lifted and he's giving me his best attempt at a dirty look, but his eyes are the color of terror.

"Get a fucking room," I say before storming off.

I'm losing it.

I've got to get out of here.

"Dude, what was that about?" Vin asks, chuckling. "You okay, man?"

No. I'm not okay.

"Yeah. Just going to grab some air for a sec." I point to the front door. If they're lucky, I'll come back. I have half a mind to call it an early night before I make a jackass out of myself again—not that I honestly give a fuck what people think about me at the end of the day. But those two were having themselves a time and the last thing they needed was some drunk bastard interrupting them.

I head out the front door and tug it closed, stepping outside to let the brisk air slap some sense into me. I exhale a clouded breath and head to the porch swing to my left—only it's occupied.

"Irie," I say when I see the unmistakable outline of her face in the dim night. She's illuminated by street lights and the glow of the garage lights, but it's her.

This time I'm fucking certain.

"How long have you been out here?" I ask. It feels like forever ago we were sitting out back, having a talk before going our separate ways, but for all I know that was ten minutes ago. My concept of time always gets glitchy when I've been drinking.

"Not long," she says, nodding toward the street. "Just waiting for the bus."

"You're leaving?"

"Yep."

I check the time on my phone. "It's only ten."

"And your point?" She half laughs through her nose before scooting over and making room for me on the porch.

"Why aren't you inside? I saw they were passing out tequila shots a little bit ago."

How I missed her walking past the main room, I'm not sure.

"Looked like you were having a good time," she says. "Taking selfies and whatnot ..."

I roll my eyes as I take the spot beside her. The chair swings back with my weight and I lean my arm over her lap, grabbing the arm rest to brace myself while also making sure she doesn't topple out. Not that she would. She isn't shit-faced like me.

"What are you going to do the rest of the night?" I ask.

"Going to bed," she says. "Nothing that would excite you."

"Now that's where you're wrong."

"Going to bed excites you?"

"*You* plus a bed excites me," I say, accidentally slurring.

Irie tilts her head. "If you're trying to be smooth, I have to be honest, Talon, it's not going well for you."

I drag in a long, icy breath and let it go before smirking. "Appreciate the honesty. Liquid confidence is a hell of a thing."

"How much have you had to drink tonight? Besides the tequila shot, I mean. You weren't this drunk twenty minutes ago when we were out back."

It's only been twenty minutes?

I was way off.

"A couple of beers," I say. The can of Miller Lite in my hand is still full, verging on room temperature now. I might as well dump it. The only thing worse than warm alcohol is ... being rejected by Irie Davenport. "What is it about me that repulses you?"

Irie's gaze snaps to mine and she begins to cough,

choking on her spit. "What? I never said I was repulsed by you."

"What is it about me that sends you running?"

"Everything," she answers without hesitation. "What is it about me that makes you so relentless?"

"Everything."

Irie shakes her head, turning away so I can't see her expression. I don't know if she's flattered or frustrated. I also don't know if I'm sober enough to tell the difference.

"My entire life, I've never been allowed to accept failure," I tell her. "It's not an option. You try or you die trying. Those are the only options."

"So you're going to die trying to hook up with me?" she asks, a hint of sarcasm in her voice.

"I'm not good at giving up, Irie," I say. "I've never worked my ass off for something and then walked way without it. I'm not a quitter. I literally don't know how to quit."

"Then you should try," she says, matter of fact. "Try to learn how to quit."

It takes everything I have not to kiss that smart mouth of hers, but I know what she's saying. She has a point—one that I'm not ready to acknowledge.

"This isn't a game to me," she tells me.

"It isn't a game to me either."

"Then why does it feel that way? Why does it feel like I'm being hunted for sport?" Her eyes rest deep on mine.

"First time I saw you, we were at a house party. Freshman year. Second weekend in October. You were wearing this white sleeveless dress with buttons down the front," I say. "It stopped a few inches above your knees. And you had these strappy sandals—tan leather, I think they were. Your hair was all the way down your back, stick straight. Bounced when you walked. And you had this wet, glossy pout that just ..." I bite my lower lip, my mouth watering just thinking about the archived image in my head.

"Why are you telling me this?"

"I'm just saying, the first time I saw you, I literally stopped in my tracks. It was like a scene in a movie where everything fades into the background. All I saw was you."

"Okay. You were a horny nineteen-year-old and you saw a pretty girl at a party and decided you wanted to screw her," she summarizes.

"Yes," I say. "And when I tried talking to you and you wanted nothing to do with me, I couldn't get you out of my head."

"Poor thing."

"And then I saw you again," I say. "Later that week. On campus. You were filling your water bottle at a fountain in Cherney Hall. Only it wasn't your water bottle. I watched as you turned and handed it to some girl sitting on a bench. The girl was crying and you crouched down beside her. You put your hand on her shoulder and told her she was going to be okay."

Irie licks her lips, staring ahead, quiet for a moment. "She was in my English class. She'd just found out a close friend passed away back home."

"Next time I saw you, you were sitting outside Briar Hall on a white blanket and you were meditating. Of all things. Meditation. Right there in the open. The sun was shining. The wind was blowing your hair around your shoulders. All around you people were moving, walking, biking by, whatever. And there you were. Completely in the moment and not giving a flying fuck what anyone thought," I say.

"A lot of people meditate."

"Not like that. And not here. Not at a school where worrying about what people think of you is pretty much a graduation requirement."

"Do you meditate?" she asks.

I pause. No one's ever asked me that. "Before games. Yeah."

Always in private. Always behind closed doors.

"The last thing I need before a big game is to get shit from one of my teammates," I say. "It's all about getting all that shit out of your head before, not carrying it out onto the field with you."

"I ... I didn't think you were into that," she says.

"There are a lot of things that would surprise you about me," I say, voice low and soft as I turn to her. "I think you and I ... we're more alike than different."

Her chest rises and falls and her fingertips twitch, dancing slightly against her thighs. I'd give the whole fucking world to know what she's thinking.

"The first time I saw you," she says a moment later. "You were heading to class. It was the first week actually. I had no idea who you were—I mean, that you played football here. Some guy came up and tried to talk to you and you literally ignored him. I think he wanted a picture? And you laughed at him and kept walking."

I swallow the hard lodge in the center of my throat.

I remember that moment. I was late for class on the other side of campus, I'd just had my ass chewed by my coach about some play I didn't study up on, and the last thing I wanted was to be bothered for a picture. The twerp even jumped out in front of me—almost made me trip over him, not so much as an "Excuse me."

"The second time I saw you," Irie continues, "was at the party. When you were hitting on me. You walked over to me like I was this sure thing, that you were supposed to smile a bit and say a few charming things and I was supposed to let you throw me over your shoulder caveman-style and carry me off to some bedroom upstairs. I think you even told me you were a psychology major and you wanted to try to figure me out."

I laugh.

She isn't wrong.

I was also drunk as fuck.

"But the third time, Talon," she says, "you were getting up in some guy's face—one of your teammates I think because he looked like a linebacker. And you were telling him what a worthless piece of shit he was, that he should give up his spot on the team to someone who actually deserves it."

It's true.

I remember that day.

His name was Matt Greene and he ended up dropping out that semester.

I was going off on him because we were roommates and I caught him coming home one day with a brown paper bag filled with syringes and vials of steroids.

If you can't play with integrity, then don't fucking play.

"The fourth time—" she begins to say.

"—Irie, I get it. You can stop now."

"I'm just saying, the guy that I've seen and the guy sitting next to me right now are two different people," she says.

"You're right. They are," I say. "I can be an asshole, Irie. I know that. But I swear to God, this? You and me? It's genuine."

The rumble of a bus sounds in the distance.

It's almost time for her to go.

"I wish I could believe you," she says. "But at the end of the day, I know deep down it's not me you want. It's that victory you've been chasing all these years."

"It started out that way," I say.

She scoffs. "You realize there's nothing you can say that's going to convince me otherwise, right?"

"Then why don't I show you?" I ask. "Let me prove it to you."

"How?" She tucks a strand of silky hair behind one ear, brows raising as she studies me.

The rumble of the bus grows louder. I feel it in my chest, reverberating in time with the hammer of my heart against my ribcage. In my head, there's a countdown clock.

5 ... 4 ... 3 ... 2 ... 1 ...

This is it.

This is my time to shine.

I lift my hand to her face, cupping her soft cheek. She's still as a statue, our eyes holding. I'm not even certain she's breathing. She has every chance to protest, every chance to push me away, but she doesn't.

She knows what's about to happen—and she's starving for it as much as I am.

I move in, taking my time, and her eyes flutter shut.

Dragging the pad of my thumb against her full bottom lip, she shivers. Leaning in closer, closer still, I angle her mouth in the perfect position before grazing it with a tease of a kiss. While every part of me wants to claim her, punish her for playing hard to get all these years, I want her to enjoy this.

I want to enjoy this.

I bring my other hand to the side of her face and guide her closer, our lips pressing together harder as our kiss becomes less restrained. Within seconds, our tongues caress and her body softens with my touch. I breathe her in—icy air and exotic flowers—and just as I'm about to pull her into my lap, the rumble of the bus turns into the screeching of brakes.

Irie pulls away, eyes wide and lips beginning to swell. "I have to go."

I reach for her arm to ask her to stay, but it's too late.

She's already trotting down the sidewalk to catch her ride home.

I watch her board and find a seat halfway down the middle before the bus drones away.

Leaning, I stretch my arms over the back of the porch swing and gather in a generous lungful of January night, every part of me electrified as I replay that moment in my head again and again.

I kissed Irie Davenport.

I kissed Irie Davenport.

And I'm going to kiss her again.

CHAPTER 9

Irie

MY LIPS ARE STILL on fire the second I walk into Aunt Bette's. The bus ride was a blink-and-it's-over eleven minutes, but I must have replayed that kiss a hundred times already. I swear I can still taste his cinnamon tongue, still feel the soft tease of his mouth grazing mine, and something tells me I'll be feeling it still come tomorrow morning.

"Irie, is that you?" Aunt Bette calls from the living room.

I peer through the doorway, toward the dark void that flickers with the flash of late-night TV commercials.

"No, it's Clark Gable," I tease back, hanging my purse on the back of a kitchen chair.

Bette makes her way from the next room. "Smart ass."

I pour myself a glass of ice water.

"Thought you were going to a party. Why are you home so early?" she asks.

"Early? It's almost eleven." I take a quick drink.

My mind replays the kiss—again, complete with the bus brakes screeching behind us. I took them as a warning sign to get the hell out of there, to pump the brakes before I let myself get carried away.

"I'd ask if you met any cute guys, but obviously you wouldn't be here if you did," Aunt Bette says, one hand on her robe-covered hip. Her hair is in curlers and her red-framed glasses almost hide the ornery grin in her eyes.

"Right. Not a one," I say. I take another sip of ice water but I still feel him, still taste him.

She squints, coming closer as she studies me. "Wait a minute. I know that look. You're lying."

"No idea what you're talking about ..."

"Your cheeks are all flushed and you're all fidgety," she says, examining me from head to toe. "What are you not telling me? Did something happen at that party? You met someone, didn't you?"

I can't lie to Bette. She's far too seasoned, far too versed in dealing with young women to know when someone's not giving her the entire scoop, so I exhale. "I didn't meet someone. I ran into someone."

She lifts a skinny brow. "Someone who's evidently made you all hot and bothered."

Bette points to the kitchen table before taking a seat. I take the one beside her, knowing there's no getting out of this.

"What's his name?" she asks.

"Talon."

"Is he handsome?"

I furrow my brow. "Yeah, but—"

"Does he have nice breath?" she asks.

I chuckle. "Yes."

"Is he nice?"

"Only when he wants to be ..." I roll my eyes.

"Is he nice to *you*?"

I bite my lip. "Yeah."

"Does he want to date you?" she asks.

"More than anything in the world."

Aunt Bette slaps her wrinkled, elfin hand on the table, shocking the life into me for a moment. "Then what on God's green earth are you doing at home? With me? Right now? You should be out with him! Having the time of your life!"

She yanks her glasses off her face, her hands flailing as she talks. I've never seen her this worked up about anything, ever.

"What's this about, Aunt Bette?"

"Would it kill you to live a little, Irie? My God. It's not like I'm going to run back and tell your aunt and uncle you went out and had yourself some fun." She buries her face in her hands.

I don't bother telling her that I'm pretty sure they don't give a rat's ass what I'm up to these days anyway. When Bette made her offer, they couldn't ship me out here fast enough. After high school, I was no longer their problem.

"You're almost twenty-three years old," Bette says, pointing her glasses at me. "You have no husband. No kids. No bills. You're never going to be as beautiful as you are right now, and I don't say that to be harsh. It's common knowledge. Once you hit thirty, your metabolism turns to shit and gravity makes everything just ... hang."

With that, I rise from the table, laughing through my nose. "All right. I'm going to go to bed now. Thanks for the pep talk, Aunt Bette."

"I'm serious, Irie." She turns in her chair as I head for the hall. "Live it up while you can. You won't regret it. And if you do, well, regrets always make for good stories at parties."

"Goodnight," I call out.

I can't deny Aunt Bette's valid argument, but I also can't throw four years out the window all because the man can kiss just as well as he can throw a football—maybe even better.

I'm stronger than that.

Even if I'm currently having a moment of weakness.

CHAPTER 10

Talon

"TALON, GOOD. YOU'RE HERE." Coach Jackson waves me into his office, where a silver-haired man with bronze skin sips coffee as he scans the wall full of plaques and trophies Monday morning. He called me while I was on my way to Anthro and told me to get here immediately, so this better be good. "Talon, this is Jerry Quick. Scout for the Richmond Hawks."

The man turns from Jackson's Wall of Fame and extends his right hand toward mine. "Talon, wow. What a pleasure to finally meet you in person. Been watching you play for a long time."

I meet his grip with mine. He squeezes hard. I squeeze harder.

"Why don't we have a seat?" Coach points to the sofa and chair set up in the corner.

A moment later, we're all situated. Jerry won't stop

blinding me with his 3D smile and Coach's knee won't stop bouncing.

"All right, I'm going to cut to the chase here," Jerry says, producing a manila folder and splaying it open on the table between us. "We'd like to sign you."

I reach for the paperwork, pulling it close to read over the terms, and I maintain my best poker face as I re-read the numbers.

Four years.

Thirty-five million plus incentives.

Jerry chuckles. "Just so you know, I had to pull a few strings. It's a little more than they were wanting to give you, but Jackson here tells me you've been holding out for something more along these lines."

I've received eight other offers since last fall, none of them half as impressive as this.

"Congratulations, Talon," Coach says, beaming. Coach never beams. He knows this is an offer I can't refuse. "Twenty years coaching and I've never seen an offer like this. Matter of fact, twenty years coaching and I've never seen a player like this either. Smashing records left and right. Makes sense your first pro offer would blow us all away."

Jerry places a shiny gold pen on the table. Does he seriously expect me to sign on the dotted line without talking to anyone first?

I check the time on my watch.

Irie's probably wondering where I am—or maybe not.

Rising, I tuck the contract into my bag and extend my hand. "Thanks, Jerry. I'll have my agent give this a look and we'll get back to you."

Jerry and Coach exchange looks. I'm sure they think I'm

a fucking moron for not sealing this in blood ASAP, but that's the last of my concerns.

I head out of the building, calling my agent on the way. I realize this is the moment I've worked for, the moment I've been waiting for my entire life—and it isn't half as exhilarating as kissing Irie.

I should be reeling. I should be walking on a fucking cloud, big dick energy and all of that.

But I feel numb, indifferent.

That kiss though?

That kiss was fire.

CHAPTER 11

Irie

THE CHAIR beside me is empty and I check my email once again. Maybe he's sick? Or maybe he kissed me and changed his mind on the whole wanting me thing? Not that I care. Not that it matters ...

I haven't stopped thinking about Saturday night. And not just the kiss. I keep thinking about all the things he said, the way his sideways glances and arrogant smirks made my stomach do flips, his blatant and unapologetic desire.

I scan the packed auditorium. It's possible he ran into someone he knew and decided to sit with them today—which is fine. But I don't see him.

It's half past eight. If he isn't here yet, he's not coming.

Professor Longmire flicks off the overhead lights and switches on the projector, clicking through a few slides until he comes to one of some ancient Mayan maps.

One of the doors down front swings open, and a strapping figure strides up the stairs, heading for the back row.

Within seconds, he makes his way closer, squeezing past tiny desks with pencil-thin computers and stepping over backpacks until he takes the spot beside me.

"Hey," I whisper to Talon.

"Hey," he whispers as he retrieves his pen and notebook. "I miss anything?"

I point to the page and a half of notes in front of me and try to focus on the lecture. The nagging voice of reason in my head is chiding me, slating me for being so concerned with his reasons for not being here.

I shouldn't have cared and it shouldn't have mattered.

Still, being this close to Talon makes Saturday night's memories come to life again. My throat constricts. My stomach tightens. I find myself stealing side glimpses of his hands, remembering the way they felt in my hair for those short-lived, sensual seconds.

By the time Longmire finishes his lecture and his TA gets the lights, it's time to pack up and head to the next class. I gather my things and turn to Talon to let him know I'll type up my notes and email them to him later today … only he's on his phone.

His back is to me and he's completely preoccupied.

This is new.

Normally he's chasing after me, using any and every excuse he can to keep our conversation going for as long as possible.

Hoisting my bag over my shoulder, I book it out of there and head to Meyer Hall, though the strangest of sensations washes over me along the way.

Disappointment, perhaps?

No.

No, that's not possible.

I'm not feeling disappointed. I won't allow it.

I should be relieved right now. I should be relieved that he's losing interest in me for whatever reason. I should be relieved that he's probably becoming someone else's problem for the rest of the semester.

Several minutes later, I find a spot in my Interior Lighting class and get settled. The disappointment that flooded my senses a short while ago has finally dissipated, only I've yet to experience any actual relief.

The only thing I'm feeling right now is foolish.

I can't believe I spent the entire weekend thinking about him, fantasizing about the teeniest, tiniest possibility of maybe, maybe, *maybe* giving him a chance.

This is what I get for having a weak moment.

And honestly, I knew better.

CHAPTER 12

Talon

"HE'S SO upset right now. You have no idea," my mother says from the other side of the phone. "The fact that he had to find out through the grapevine and not from his own son?"

Stepson ...

I hoist my bag over my shoulder. I'm not going to apologize. I was literally presented with the offer one hour ago, called my agent, and booked it to class.

"Nothing's finalized yet," I say. "I didn't want to make any announcements until it was official."

"That's not the point," she scoffs in true Camilla Masterson fashion. It's not easy being half martyr, half victim, and full-blooded drama queen. "The point is Mark should have been the first person you called, not Ira."

She's seriously mad at me for calling my agent before calling my stepdad?

I can't with her.

Not today.

"I think you should plan on coming home tonight," she says. "I'll make dinner reservations at Miato's to celebrate and you can apologize to your father then. After all, none of this would have happened if it weren't for him."

Well aware ...

We all know Mark's dreams of pro football stardom went up in smoke when he tore his ACL playing in college. Never quite made a full recovery, never got over it, so he had to live vicariously through me.

At the end of the day, my scholarship—and this contract—are his.

I'm nothing more than a football-throwing machine, an avatar for his overinflated ego.

People joke about Tiger Woods and how his father aggressively pushed him from a young age and shaped him into the golf club wielding champion he is today.

Mark Masterson would make Earl Woods look like Mary fucking Poppins.

"I can't do tonight, Mom," I lie. "I need more notice than that."

"Fine," she says. "This Friday. I know you don't have any classes in the afternoon so that should give you plenty of time to make your way down for the night. Why don't we plan on seven?"

"Yeah. Sure." I glance up and find a mostly-empty auditorium.

Shit.

Irie's long gone.

I was hoping to ask her if she could send her notes to me from the first half of class.

"Hey, Mom. I've got to go," I say.

"Okay, but don't forget to call Mark," she says. "I mean

it. Call him as soon as you can. Explain to him why you didn't tell him first and then tell him you're coming home Friday to celebrate."

"Yep." I end the call and make my way outside, but not before emailing Irie to ask about the notes—and to secure another study date for Thursday night.

CHAPTER 13

Irie

HE BROUGHT A BLANKET.

And coffee.

I find him in a cozy corner of the greenspace in front of the library Thursday evening, camped out on a black and white buffalo check blanket.

This is supposed to be a study date, but the only thing studious about it is the notebook in his lap and pen behind his ear.

"Irie, hi," he says when I take a seat across from him. He hands me a white paper cup and a spare sweatshirt. "It's supposed to get cold."

"You know we're only doing this for a half hour, right?" I ask, fighting a half-smirk. I'm charmed. I am. I won't lie. But it doesn't excuse the hot-and-coldness this week.

We shared that kiss on Saturday. On Monday he came to class late and barely said two words to me, though he did shoot me an email asking about notes. During Wednesday's lecture, he was still quiet—though he did walk out with me and remind me of our standing study date.

Maybe this isn't as fun for him anymore? Maybe since I let him kiss me, the chase is slowing down and it isn't that exciting? The cheetah has finally caught up to the gazelle and now he's bored.

"Thanks for this," I say, sipping my coffee, which I now realize is a mocha cappuccino ... which just so happens to be my favorite. I'm not even going to ask how he knew. He'll probably go on some tangent about the eleventh time he saw me in a coffee shop or something. "You doing okay?"

He peers at me through squinted eyes. "Of course. Why do you ask?"

"You haven't been ..." I gather a lungful of air. "You haven't been yourself this week. After the kiss, I thought you'd be ..."

He doesn't say a word, he simply lets me continue on, stumbling over my words and digging myself into a hole that shows I actually kind of maybe give a damn.

"*Oh*," he says a second later, eyes lit. "You thought I backed off because we kissed last weekend and I lost interest."

"Warn a girl before you read her mind, will you?"

"I haven't told anyone yet," he begins to say, scooting in closer and narrowing the space between us. "But I was offered a pro contract this week."

"Ah. Congratulations."

I'm happy for him. I am. On a human to human level, I know how hard he's worked and how much he deserves something to show for that. But this proves my point—it was never about me. It was about the chase. And at the end of the semester, he's going to move far away from here and never look back. He's going to be some multi-millionaire baller and I'm going to be nothing more than a blip on his college timeline.

And I'm fine with that.

I am.

Or I *will* be ...

Sometimes it's nice being right.

Other times it stings a bit.

"I haven't signed anything yet," he says. "We're still in the negotiation stage. But there are a lot of phone calls and back and forth. So if I've seemed preoccupied lately ..."

"Talon, it's fine." I wave him away.

"Obviously it's not if you're bringing it up," he says.

"I just thought, maybe, at some point we should address the kiss, that's all."

"All right, fine. I'll go first," he says. "I can't stop thinking about it."

I'm mid-sip of my coffee and he's lucky I didn't spit it out all over him.

"You have the softest lips I've ever tasted," he adds. "And I really wish you wouldn't have run off to catch that fucking bus."

I glance down, away. I wasn't expecting him to say any of that. I was hoping we could agree that it was nice and that it shouldn't happen again, that we could be adults and "study buddies" and get through the rest of the semester now that we got that out of our system.

I peer up at him, speechless, my pathetic ego wishing it could hear him say those things one more time.

"You're shivering," he says, situating his sweatshirt over my lap.

It isn't the cold making me shiver, but I don't tell him that.

His fingertips trace my knee and my skin flashes hot. It's

funny how something so small can overpower me, reducing my resolve to rubble.

"Now it's my turn to ask if you're okay ..."

"Of course," I say, forcing myself to snap out of it. I need to pull myself together. "Maybe we should study now?"

"No," he says, examining me. "I told you how I felt about the kiss, but you didn't tell me how you felt."

My lips part but no sound comes out. I shrug, letting my hands fall in my lap, on his ridiculously soft PVU sweatshirt that smells like him.

"It was nice," I manage a moment later.

"Just nice?" He scratches his left temple.

"Yeah. It was nice, but I think it was a one-and-done kind of thing," I say. "We got it out of our systems."

"Did we though?"

My cheeks flush. What is it about this man that makes me a bundle of nervous energy? No one else—and I mean no one else—brandishes this kind of physical influence over me.

"I didn't," he says, voice low. "I didn't get you out of my system. Not even close."

"We really need to get on track here." I check my watch.

"Why won't you give this a chance?"

"Give *what* a chance?"

"This."

"What do you mean by *this*? You're going to have to be more specific," I say.

"You and me," he says, careful not to use labels. He's strategic, which serves him well on the field I'm sure, but in real life, it's infuriating.

I burrow my trembling hands in the folds of his sweatshirt, my mind and body and heart waging an epic battle on the inside.

"Tell me what it's going to take to tear down this fucking fortress you've built around yourself," he says. "And while you're at it, tell me who put it there so I can kick his fucking ass."

He manages a sniffled chuckle out of me.

But if he only knew ...

"I appreciate the chivalry, but we really should start studying," I say, retrieving my materials from my bag. "I have to catch the bus in a half hour."

"One date," he says.

My gaze flicks to his as I click the end of my pen. "Talon."

"Give me one date and if it's the worst date of your life ... I'll never bother you again," he says. "I swear on my life. On my *career*."

Before I realize it, I've already spoken the words, "I'll think about it."

Talon's mouth curls wide and his eyes flash, and without saying another word, without pushing it, he grabs his notebook and begins quizzing me on the week's topics.

There he goes, tackling my self-control, dominating the game like he does so well, and I have no one to blame but myself.

I'm letting him win.

The only question ... why?

CHAPTER 14

Talon

"TAKE IT EASY, Tal. You don't want to show up with a beer gut your first week," my stepdad says Friday night at Miato's in Laguna Cove. "You're still hitting the gym every day, right?"

I drove two hours here per my mother's request, all so I could partake in some bullshit celebration of my contract, which is really a roundabout celebration for Mark.

Mark reaches over, wrapping a chubby hand around my bicep before poking at my non-existent belly.

I wonder what he'd do if I poked his?

The bastard would probably shit himself. He's not used to anyone pointing out any of his flaws. In his own mind, he's rich, successful, and perfect in ways other men can only dream about. He lives in a self-made bubble of inflated confidence.

One of these days I intend to burst it.

But I won't do it here or now, in front of my mother.

"Come on, you two," Mom says, sipping her champagne and laughing like we're just a couple of guys razzing each other, never mind the fact that Mark's the one making the comments. I'm keeping my mouth shut, like I always do, for her sake. I swear I haven't seen this much light in her eyes since I got my full ride football scholarship to PVU. It wasn't like they couldn't have afforded my tuition or I couldn't have taken out loans and paid for college myself. It wasn't about any of that. It was that they wanted the bragging rights. They wanted that validation that the football camps and thousand-dollar-an-hour coaches and rigorous, year-round training schedules were worth it. "We're here to have a good time now."

I glance across the table at my teenage stepsisters, Hadley and Kelsey, their noses buried in the glow of their iPhones and virgin martinis resting in front of their untouched entrees.

Mom keeps placing her hand on Mark's shoulder, leaning over and kissing him like they're celebrating some monumental anniversary or lottery win. She can't stop smiling. He can't take that smug smile off his face to save his life.

"Talon, I hope you know your father would be so, so proud of you right now." Mom's voice strains and her eyes water and her hand moves to her throat as she chokes off tears. She normally only gets this way after three glasses of *champs*, not one. I'm guessing she engaged in a little celebratory pre-drinking before they left the house.

"Yes, he sure would be," Mark echoes. "God rest his soul."

The only time, and I mean the *only* time, Mark acts like he gives a rat's ass about my dead father is when my mother gets sentimental, and then he has to play the role of the supportive second husband.

But Mark couldn't care less.

He didn't know my dad. Not on a personal level. My dad was an architect and Mark was a one-time client, commissioning a commercial office space building from him when I was six. My father was a bit older than my mother, who was strikingly beautiful in a timeless sort of way in her younger years, long before the Botox and implants and the things she felt she had to do to her body to look the part of Mark's Orange County wife.

Fake lips.

Silicone boobs.

A plastic soul to encapsulate the authentic one she buried along with my father.

The two of them met at a group for grieving spouses, Mark having just lost his wife when she swerved off a cliff to avoid hitting a deer. His girls were just babies then. They needed a mom. And Mark needed money, seeing how he and his wife were too broke to spend a few hundred bucks a year on life insurance policies.

Mark took one look at my mother, at my lonely, grief-stricken, shell of a woman mother, and an opportunity was born. I was young then but I still remember the day he moved in with us. How happy my mother was. How much life was in her eyes again. She told me I was going to be a big brother, that I was going to have a dad again.

Over the first few years, Mark was the very definition of a doting father. He taught me how to throw a football, swing a golf club, and cast a fishing reel. But the fun and games ended as soon as he realized how naturally athletic I was and decided he wanted me to fulfill his dream of playing pro football.

At first, it was nice—the special coaches and clinics, all

the accolades and glory and attention—but after a while, it got old.

All my friends were living it up, running around being stupid teenagers and doing stupid teenage shit.

Me? I was in bed by eight every night so I could meet up with my trainer by five the next morning. God forbid I didn't get an hour in every morning before school with the guy that was going to "help make our dreams come true."

After a while, I was in too deep.

I was too damn good.

The attention was insane and it became my identity.

High school blurred into football, and soon I was leading the PVU Tigers as their starting quarterback, which came with a whole new level of attention and accolades.

But I'll never forget sitting down with Mark my senior year of high school, telling him I wanted to be done with football. I thanked him for everything, told him I appreciated everything he'd done, but I wanted to enjoy my college experience without the stress of always having to be number one.

I thought he'd be cool about it.

He'd always been cool about everything …

But I swear to God, the man's eyes turned pitch black and he hooked a hand on my shoulder, squeezing until a shock of pain flooded my muscles, and he told me, point blank, that if I didn't play football, he'd leave my mother.

I laughed at first.

I thought he was joking.

What would me playing football have to do with his marriage?

But the more I thought about it, the more I realized, he didn't need her any more. With the help of my father's life insurance money, he'd grown his little real estate business into a multi-million-dollar corporation—and his daughters weren't babies any more.

He didn't need my mother.

He could walk away a rich man, find someone younger, more exciting, less Xanax and wine flooding her system at any given moment.

It was me.

I was the reason he stuck around.

He wanted to live his shattered football dreams through me, and nothing was going to keep that from happening.

The bastard knew I loved my mother, that I didn't want to see her alone and devastated from losing yet another husband. So I shut my mouth. I kept up with the coaching and the clinics and the practices. And I took my spot as the PVU Tigers starting quarterback the following fall without so much as a complaint.

"Can you believe it?" Mom says, sipping from her flute. "Richmond. Who'd have thought? Mark, we might have to buy a second place in Virginia. Maybe a little condo we can use during home games?"

Mark scoffs, his bulbous belly jiggling. "Condo? Hell, I think Talon here can drop a million or two on a place for Mom and Dad, don't you?"

She chuckles, like he's the funniest fucker on the planet, and brushes her hand along his arm. "Oh, stop."

"I'm not kidding. We've probably invested half a million dollars into this kid's career," Mark says. His eyes twinkle like he's trying to keep it lighthearted for Mom's sake, but I know he's as serious as the heart attack that ripped my father's life from this world.

I ignore their bullshit banter and slide my phone from my pocket, checking my email.

Yesterday I asked Irie for one date. She told me she'd

think about it, which I'm ninety-nine percent sure means she's going to say yes—she just had to tamp down her excitement. God forbid she owns the fact that she wants me just as badly as I want her.

I press the 'refresh' button and watch the screen populate, mostly with junk emails and various campus alerts.

And then I see it.

An email from Irie.

"One date," the subject line reads. In the body of the email she's written, "Pick me up Saturday at seven. 472 Calle Blanco."

"Talon, what are you over there grinning about, huh?" Mom asks with a wink, her words half-slurred. "Did Richmond decide to sweeten the pot? I bet it drives them crazy that you haven't signed yet."

I rise, tossing my cloth napkin on my plate before rounding the table.

"Nah," I say when I get to Mom. "Nothing like that."

"Well then what is it?" she asks.

I don't tell her about Irie. Girlfriends were never a thing growing up. Mark didn't allow them. He thought they'd be too distracting and he was probably right. After a while, Mom began to echo Mark's sentiments because she believed he could do no wrong and therefore was never wrong about anything. My only taste of the finer sex was limited to house party hook-ups while Mark and Mom were on their monthly trips.

Despite the fact that I'm almost twenty-three, I've still yet to bring a girl home to meet either of them.

I might be a cruel bastard.

But I'm not *that* fucking cruel.

"Going to head back," I say, kissing my mom's glass-like forehead. "Thanks for ... this."

I glance at my stepsisters who haven't said more than two words this entire night and then to Mark, who's shooting me a look that suggests I'm an asshole for leaving *his* celebration early.

But fuck that guy.

Making my way to the valet stand, I give the kid in the red jacket my ticket and read Irie's email one more time while I wait for them to bring my car around, and when he pulls up, I tip him a twenty—partly because I'm in a fan-fucking-tastic mood and partly because Mark's only going to tip the poor soul a couple of bucks when he fetches his Rolls Royce SUV an hour from now.

"Thanks, man," the kid says as he hands me my keys.

I climb in my car, set the music for the two-hour drive ahead, and veer toward the freeway, cruising on gasoline and adrenaline.

This time tomorrow, I'm going on a date with Irie Davenport.

CHAPTER 15

Irie

"I DON'T THINK I've ever seen you curl your hair," Brynn says from my bed as I stand in front of my dresser mirror, a long-barrel curling iron in hand.

"Is it too much?" I ask.

I still can't believe I agreed to a date with Talon.

"Too much?" Brynn scoffs. "Honey, you're going on a date with Talon freaking Gold. It might not be enough. Where's the push up bra and the fuck-me heels?"

I shoot her a look from the mirror.

"I'm teasing. But seriously. Do you know how many girls would kill to be you right now?" she asks. "I mean, everyone knows he doesn't date so the fact that he wants to take you out ..."

I roll my eyes. "Lucky me, right?"

"I don't know why you're acting like you're doing this as some kind of favor to him. You're allowed to be excited. And you should be. You're going to have an amazing time tonight."

"Hopefully." I give her a wink as I curl the last section.

"Are you going to let him kiss you again?" she asks.

I shrug. "If it happens, it happens."

"What if he wants more than a kiss this time?"

I run my hand through my cooled curls to loosen them up before reaching for a tube of juicy pink lip gloss. "Then he'll be sorely disappointed."

A couple spritzes of perfume later, I examine myself in the full-length mirror in the corner. I opted for high-waisted jeans, strappy heels, and a white sweater. Definitely going for a casual look that's a touch above my normal style yet doesn't scream that I'm trying too hard.

The doorbell rings.

I gather a deep breath, grab my purse, and give myself one last once-over in the mirror before heading for the hallway.

"All right, babe. It's your time to shine," Brynn says, following behind me. "And I'm going to expect a full report first thing tomorrow."

By the time I round the corner, I can hear Aunt Bette talking near the front door. She's already let him in. Knowing her, she was probably waiting by the front window, watching for him to pull up.

"I'd tell you to bring her back the way you found her, but I'd almost rather you didn't," I hear Aunt Bette saying. "Show our girl a good time."

"Aunt Bette," I say, clearing my throat.

Talon's weighty stare lifts to mine and Aunt Bette turns on her house-slippered feet.

"Irie." Talon's lips slip into a small smile. "Wow. Look at you."

Who knew a few curls and some lip gloss would be all it takes to impress this man?

"You ready?" I ask. If we stand here any longer, Bette and Brynn are going to be popping popcorn. From the way they're gawking, you'd think they were watching a real-life Nicholas Sparks movie playing out.

Talon gets the door, giving Aunt Bette and Brynn a quick nod goodbye, and within seconds he's escorting me to an idling black BMW, every square inch of which is polished, shined, and waxed.

"I'll get that," he says, stepping around me to grab the passenger door.

I've never had a guy open a car door for me. It's strange and old-fashioned and yet ... kind of nice.

I slide into the warm, buttery leather and he makes his way to the driver's side. The radio plays some indie rock station on low and the car smells like new leather with a hint of clean soap and aftershave.

"What's the plan?" I ask when he climbs in.

"You'll find out in about fifteen minutes," he says, buckling in and checking his mirrors. "You warm enough? Music okay?"

"I am. And it is." I study him from my periphery as we drive south. If I had to guess, we're headed downtown.

The fabric of his navy cashmere sweater strains against his muscles as he drives and the silver watch on his left hand glints with each passing streetlamp. The car glides from street to street, the ride easy and smooth, and he drives like a man who isn't in any kind of rush—a man who has the entire night ahead of him and wants to savor every moment.

"What'd you do last night?" I ask.

"Had to go to Laguna Cove for a family dinner," he says.

"Is that where you're from?"

"It is." He studies the road ahead, coming to a gentle stop at the next light.

"Isn't that a couple hours from here?"

Talon nods.

"You didn't want to stay the weekend?" I ask.

He laughs through his nose. "You don't know my family. An hour-long dinner with them is about as much as I can take."

I have to admit, I'm surprised.

Talon has always projected a certain image to me and that image isn't the kind I typically associate with dysfunctional families. Everything about him screams privilege and familial support.

"What'd you do last night?" he asks.

"Went to this spoken word poetry slam thing at Café Baudelaire with a couple girls from my Interior Lighting class," I say. "First time going to one of those and I have to say … it'll probably be my last."

He laughs.

"I'm all about the art scene, but how do people keep a straight face when they're up there? This guy had this whole poem about losing his beloved … stick bug."

"Stick bug?"

"Yes. Stick bug," I say. "He had tears in his eyes and everything. I mean, I don't mean to judge. I'm just saying I can't relate and it's not my thing."

"It's good to try new things," Talon says, glancing at me as he flicks on his turn signal.

A few minutes later, he pulls into a parallel parking spot in front of a massive downtown building, one I've never seen in my life since I rarely venture off campus.

"We're here," he says before climbing out.

I don't wait for him to get my door, though I'm sure he would. I meet him on the sidewalk.

"What's this?" I ask as we head to a series of glass doors so dark you can't see in.

"It's an art exhibit," he says, placing his hand on the small of my back and guiding me inside.

We step into a wide-open space, nothing but white walls and white pillars and patrons from all walks of life making their way between stationed exhibits. Talon hands two tickets to a woman dressed in black standing behind a small podium, and then he swipes a couple of champagne glasses from a passing server's tray.

"For you." He hands me one of the flutes before scanning the room. "They hold this every year. Most of the time I come alone."

I'm confused.

And also impressed.

"I never thought of you as an art guy," I say. Taking a closer look around, I realize this isn't just art. This is some kind of architecture-art hybrid exhibit. Everything around us has to do with buildings and living spaces.

We pass a hanging banner and I stop in my tracks when I read the words: WELCOME TO THE 20th ANNUAL GOLD-HARRIS EXHIBIT.

Gold-Harris is a world-renowned local architectural firm, one we studied extensively a couple of years back in one of my design classes.

"Are you related to Theodore Gold?" I ask.

Talon takes a sip, his lips pressing flat. "Was. Was related."

I don't understand.

"He was my father," he says. "He died when I was six."

For a moment, I'm not sure I heard him correctly, so I

replay his words in my head. I'm sure to anyone else, this revelation would be no big deal, but he might as well have just told me he's architecture royalty.

"Oh, my goodness." I close my gaping mouth and try to show some respect. "I had no idea."

I didn't even know Gold had passed. They talked about his work in my class—but they never talked about his life.

"I'm so sorry," I say. "But for the record, your father's work is some of my favorite. I admire his talent immensely."

"Thank you," he says before extending his arm. "Mind if I show you around?"

I slip my hand into his, the cashmere of his sleeve soft beneath my palm, and he leads me to a wall on the left. It's a black and white photograph of a beautiful home, white and stately and symmetrical but also welcoming with its picket fence and double front doors. I lean in to take a better look and find a little boy sitting on the front steps, a calico kitten in his lap. He's grinning ear to ear, his hair wavy and hanging in his face.

The plaque beneath the image reads: "HOME." Photography by Camilla Gold-Masterson.

"Is that you?" I ask.

"It is. That was the home my father designed and had built for my mother when they got married. She's the one who took the picture." He points to a window on the top level. "That was my room."

"You had a cat."

He smiles. "We did. Her name was Turtle—because she looked like a turtle sundae."

My hand is still curled around his bicep and he leads me to the next photo. It's another image taken by Camilla Gold-Masterson. His mother must have remarried after his father's death. I try to think of Talon as a child, what that must have been like for him. Given the fact that he claimed he could hardly spend more than an hour with his family nowadays, I can only imagine it wasn't always ideal.

"Was your mom a photographer?" I ask.

He shrugs. "She dabbled. Mostly she was into interior design, remodeling, that sort of thing."

I glance around the room. "Is she here?"

"Nah." He leave sit as that and I don't pry because nothing about him gives me the impression that he wants to elaborate on it.

Talon leads me to the next image and the next, all of them photographs his mother took from various homes and projects his father had designed over the years. Some of them are familiar—I swear these images have been used in textbooks of mine.

We make our way to the next section—mostly 3D renderings of various world-famous buildings, some of which have been reimagined in the style of Picasso or Dali.

"I can't believe I've never heard of this exhibition before," I say when we get to the next section—oil paintings of local bungalows. "You'd think somewhere along the lines, one of my professors would've mentioned it."

"They hold it every year. Same place. Same week."

"And you always go?"

"Always." He tosses back the final sip of his champagne and I realize I've been so entranced with my surroundings I've barely touched mine. "I don't remember much about my father. In a way, this makes me feel closer to him."

"Did you ever think about getting into architecture?"

"I did."

"And?"

"It wasn't an option for me. The architecture program at

PVU is pretty intense. It wouldn't have worked with my football schedule."

"Talon?" An older woman with cherry red lipstick and thick glasses strides up to us. "I thought that was you!" She embraces him in a hug before reaching to cup his face in her hands. "It's so wonderful to see you. Gosh, you look more and more like your father every year."

"Irie, this is Lindee Harris. She was my father's partner at Gold-Harris," he says. "Lindee, this is Irie Davenport. She's an interior design student at PVU."

My jaw drops as she extends her hand toward mine.

"Oh, my goodness. I'm a huge fan of your work," I tell her. "The conceptual city hall design you did for the Stockton project blew my mind. And your residential work is incredible, the way you brought timeless style and modern edge to new construction was lightyears ahead of its time."

"Why, thank you, Irie. You're far too kind," she says, clasping her fingers around the diamond pendant on her neck and gifting me a humble smile. Turning to Talon, she adds, "Theodore was a major inspiration in my early days. My work wouldn't be what it is without his brutally honest guidance. Interning with him completely changed the way I approached my work and being able to start a firm with him completely changed the course of my career." Her attention skips past our shoulders and from behind, I hear someone calling for her. "Anyway, it was so good seeing you Talon, and Irie, a pleasure to meet you. If you ever want to talk shop, Talon can give you my number. Shaping young minds is a bit of a pet passion of mine."

She places a gentle hand on my shoulder before making her way to another corner of the room.

The instant she's gone, I turn to Talon, flushed and speechless.

"Are you starstruck right now?" he asks with a chuckle.

"Um, yes," I finally manage. "That's Lindee Harris. *Lindee Harris.*"

Talon laughs. "I know who it is."

"She's an architectural legend," I say. "Gold and Harris are the Simon and Garfunkel of the modern architectural movement."

"Which one's Simon and which one's Garfunkel?" he asks. "Answer carefully."

I give him a playful nudge. "Stop. You know what I mean. I'm too flustered right now to come up with a better analogy. How'd you get tickets to this on such short notice anyway? I saw a sign up front that said tonight was sold out."

"Made a phone call to one of my father's old friends ..."

We make our way down a hallway, toward another section of the show which has small exhibits set up like various rooms, all of them showcasing the importance of the marriage of functional design and interior style.

"I'm geeking out so hard right now," I say as I release my hand from his arm and grab my phone to snap a few pictures.

He stands back, hands digging in the pockets of his jeans, his eyes full of amusement as he watches my inner design nerd take the wheel.

When I'm done, he checks his watch. "We've only got a few more minutes then we need to head out. I got us a spot at the Ultra lounge."

"Wait. Ultra? As in ultra-exclusive, impossible-to-get-into Ultra?" I ask. It's not that I'm impressed by these sorts of things, but I've heard all about this place and the man must have sold the rights to his firstborn child to get us a spot there.

"That's the one." Talon hooks his arm around my waist, steering us to the next exhibit, leaning down to whisper into my ear. "Told you it'd be the best date of your life."

THERE'S a reason the Ultra lounge is impossible to get into.

Plush seats that swallow you whole.

Celebrity DJ imported from Sweden.

Top shelf liquor.

Cozy, ambient lighting.

Dimmed crystal chandeliers that sparkle just right.

First class service.

It isn't shoulder to shoulder, overly crowded, or full of college students living their best lives ... it's chill, peaceful, and ambient.

A world away.

"Ms. Davenport. Mr. Gold," our cocktail server says, depositing our drinks on glass coasters on the table before us. "I'll be back to check on you in a while. Enjoy."

She struts off and Talon hands me my drink—an Aperol spritzer.

"Cheers," he says, clinking his tumbler against my martini glass a second later.

We're surrounded by some of the most beautiful people I've ever seen, velvet everything, and the kind of music that puts you in an upscale trance—but it's the strangest thing.

All I see is him.

"How's it taste?" he asks after I take a sip of my drink.

I let the bitter orange and sweet champagne bubbles pop on my tongue before swallowing. "Like magic. Yours?"

"Best Korean ginseng whiskey I've ever had." He winks, taking a small sip.

"This place is incredible, Talon," I say, peering around the room. My attention stops by the DJ booth, where some woman in a white dress is leaning in to request a song. "That woman looks familiar. I swear I saw her on that perfume billboard on Ocean Drive. Is that ... is that ...?"

I don't finish my thought because her name escapes me, but that face—I'd recognize that face anywhere because it's everywhere.

And now it's here.

In the flesh.

"Probably." Talon shrugs, not so much as attempting to follow my gaze. "So ..."

"Yes?"

"I told you a little about me back at the gallery, about my family," he says. "Tell me about yours. You're from the Midwest, right?"

"Missouri," I say, reaching for the wooden drink menu on the table. "And I highly suggest we find a more enthralling topic of conversation."

"Your parents, tell me about them," he says, ignoring my suggestion.

"My mom isn't an interior designer and my dad isn't a famous architect," I say with a wink. "That's about all I can say about them."

The music pulses behind us, slow and steady, but my heart is rapid-firing. Talking about my family always gets me worked up, but I'm trying to keep this moment light. Discussing those two will only weigh it down.

"Come on," he says, half-laughing. "I'm being serious. I

want to know all about you, where you came from, what got you here."

I take a generous sip of my spritzer and fold the drink menu before pushing it aside. "I don't usually talk about that. With anyone."

"I don't talk about my father either," he says. "But honestly, it felt kind of good talking about him with you earlier."

I exhale. It's been years since I've talked about my parents, but maybe it could do me some good to unload some of that baggage? Besides, it's not like my crazy family is going to send him running. It's not like he's interviewing the future mother of his child and trying to ensure his future prodigy won't be tainted with wacko blood.

I decide to give him the condensed version.

"I've never met my father," I say. "And my mother lives on some commune in Idaho that doesn't believe in electronics and like to pretend they're still living in the pioneer days."

Talon almost chokes on his whiskey.

"Since the age of ten, I was shipped from family member to family member until I was thirteen and my mom's brother and his wife took me in." I take another drink because I'm going to need it. "I spent my teenage years living in the strictest household in the entire state of Missouri by an aunt and uncle who were convinced I was the spawn of Satan because they caught me listening to Selena Gomez once."

"That nuts, huh?"

I lift my palm. "Hand to God. I couldn't get out of there fast enough and they couldn't get rid of me fast enough."

I leave out a few other details, things that are neither here nor there and not worth repeating—at least not now.

"So how'd you end up here?" he asks.

"Aunt Bette," I say. "Though technically she's not my aunt. She's my uncle's wife's aunt. But she needed a live-in caretaker, and she offered to take me in and pay for my schooling if I lived with her. And so I did."

"You happy you did?" he asks. "Can't imagine you're getting the full college experiencing living off-campus."

"I couldn't care less about the full college experience," I say, taking a swig. It's mostly true. Sometimes I look at people who are able to live so carelessly and carefree and I get that pang of jealousy, but then I look at Aunt Bette—who isn't even technically part of my family and yet she treats me like I'm her own. Out of everyone, she's the truest family member I've ever known.

"Your aunt was telling me to make sure you had a good time tonight," he says.

I laugh into my martini glass. "Of course she was. First time I met her, she gave me a peach wine cooler and sat me down to relive her glory days as a strip club manager."

"No shit?"

"I shit you not."

"Just checking in," our cocktail waitress appears out of nowhere. "Can I get you anything?"

We order another round—plus shots—and settle in, our bodies warm and pliable and melting against the impossibly soft velvet seating we share.

She returns within minutes, placing our drinks in a perfect row, and Talon hands me one of the shot glasses.

"To our date," he says, making a toast. "Hopefully the first of many more to come."

Our glasses clink and I toss mine back. It burns like fire on the way down and I wipe a rogue drop from the corner of my mouth with my pinky. Talon watches my every move, and now that I think about it, he's hardly taken his eyes off me all night.

It's funny ... when I look at him tonight, I don't see the arrogant quarterback, the man obsessed with screwing me. I don't see the cruel Adonis with the corded steel muscles and permanent scowl.

I see a man: a devilishly attractive man who knows how to craft a night I'm never going to forget as long as I live.

The DJ spins a new track, this one slower, more repetitious, undeniably sensual. Without thinking, I find myself staring at his mouth. My throat turns dry as I try to swallow the anxious lump that forms. The flurry of butterflies in my middle are quickly overpowered by the ricochet of my heart hammering against my ribcage.

Leaning back, Talon settles into the sofa we share before casually wrapping his arm around the backrest. His body heat radiates onto me and his citrus-woods cologne fills my lungs. My tongue zings with the anticipation of his cinnamon taste.

He's going to kiss me again.

I *feel* it.

The buildup ...

The anticipation ...

Drawing in a careful breath, I pace my whirring thoughts and try to relax, try to place myself in this moment where the outside world doesn't exist, where yesterday is irrelevant and tomorrow is unwritten.

The song changes again—which marks four minutes of Talon not making a move on me. I glance over at him and he shoots a half-smirk that sets my nerve endings ablaze. With as subtle an effort as I can muster, I bite my lower lip, thinking maybe a hint might move things along ... but four minutes pass and a new song plays.

Talon clears his throat, stretching his arms behind his head and getting re-situated.

"I was thinking," he begins to say, "do you—"

He doesn't get a chance to finish.

Icy cold liquid spills down the side of my head, dripping down my shoulder, and careening down the front of my white sweater. In the ambient lighting, I can't tell if it's purple, red, or blue, but it's definitely not water.

"Oh my God!" A woman shrieks behind me. "I'm *so* sorry!"

Talon is quick to rise and even quicker to my side. "Jesus, Irie. You okay?"

"Yeah," I say, still in shock. He shoots the woman a look, his lips ready as if he's about to say something, and then our server appears with a handful of cloth napkins.

"These heels," the woman says, pointing at her feet. "Still breaking them in. Clumsy me."

I turn to take a look at her for myself, only to find the coyest of smiles on her mouth.

She did this on purpose.

"Bullshit, Alicia," Talon says, confirming my suspicions. "The fuck is wrong with you?"

The Alicia chick scoffs before redirecting her attention to me. "I said it was an accident."

Talon snatches one of the napkins from the server, dabbing it against the sticky sweet mess that has become my ruined curls.

"It's okay," I say, taking it from him. "I've got it."

"I'd be happy to get some new drinks going for you all," the server says, but Talon doesn't hear it. The music is pumping and he's going off on the girl who spilled the drink.

"I'm going to the ladies' room," I say, but no one hears me. People stare as I make my way to the back of the lounge, but I do my best to ignore them. Once inside the rest room, I take a look at my reflection and the splash of cosmo-pink liquor across my white top. I run my fingers through my tangled hair, which is already beginning to reek of dried, sugary alcohol, and try to comb it into place but with little success, so I grab a hair tie from my bag and wrap it into a low, messy bun.

It's not perfect, but it just might salvage the night—and I want it to.

I've been enjoying myself and I'm not quite ready to go home yet.

I return to our reserved sofa a few minutes later.

Talon's already signing the check.

"They're not kicking us out, are they?" I ask.

He glances up, placing the pen down. "Nah. Figured we could use a change of scenery after that … incident."

"So you knew her?" I ask, turning to point to a girl who is clearly long gone.

His nose twitches. "Unfortunately."

On that note, we leave Ultra. I don't ask any more questions about Alicia and he doesn't say another word, and it's for the best. Bullies are only powerful when you give them power over you.

She doesn't get to ruin this night.

"Mind if we walk around a bit?" he asks once we're outside.

"Of course not."

A gush of tepid wind blows my damp hair over my shoulder as we stroll the downtown sidewalks of Pacific Valley, but I brush it away. We don't get more than a couple of blocks before Talon slips his hand in mine and pulls me against him.

"You must be freezing in that," he says glancing at my

damp sweater before nodding toward a retail store ahead. "Why don't we get you something clean?"

Before I have a chance to respond, he takes my hand and leads me through the double doors of an upscale women's clothing boutique—one I wouldn't have dreamt of setting foot in before.

"It's fine," I say. I'd rather be damp and cold than slap down a line like, "I can't afford anything in here," because I know what he'll do and I don't need him to do that. Plus it's late. The sign on the door indicates that they close in fifteen minutes. I don't want to be *that* customer.

"Don't be stubborn. Just grab something you like. My treat," he says. "If I hadn't have taken you to Ultra, you wouldn't be in this position in the first place."

I stand in the middle of a store filled with shoes and bags and jackets that cost more than some people make in a month, paralyzed with indecision.

"Fine," Talon says. "I'll make it easy for you."

He walks to a rack and plucks a leopard-print cashmere sweater off the rack—medium—a safe choice. A correct one too.

"You like it?" he asks.

I reach for the price tag but he yanks it away.

"I'll take that as a yes." With that, Talon carries it to the cash register, where a short-haired woman with hair the color of the unstained parts of my current sweater gives us a curious gaze. When she begins to box it up, Talon tells her to stop. "She'll wear it out."

The woman cuts the tags and begins to hand the sweater to him, but he steps back, pointing at me.

"Please show her to a changing room," he says.

The white-haired woman leads me to a small room with a curtain for a door and hands me the priceless sweater before disappearing. Tearing off my wet, ruined top, I tug the new one over my head and adjust it into place. Next, I manage to find a spare elastic in the bottom of my purse and twist my hair into a low, messy bun. On top of that, I happen to spot a tube of vintage red lipstick in a side pocket. I almost swipe it across my lips when I stop myself. No man in his right mind wants to kiss a girl and walk away looking like a clown.

Giving myself a final once-over in the mirror, I rub my palms against the sugar-soft material. If cotton candy clouds were sweaters, this is exactly what they'd feel like.

I will cherish this sweater for the rest of my life, I'm sure of it. Long after it's out of style, it'll still be hanging from a velvet hanger in the back of my closet, a souvenir of this night and everything it entailed.

I place the lipstick back in my purse along with the old sweater, and then I step out from behind the curtain. Talon's seated in a white leather arm chair, reading something on his phone, when he glances up, wasting no time drinking me in from bottom to top.

"Ready?" I ask.

He rises, sliding his phone back into his pocket.

"All right. Good as new." He takes my hand and leads me outside, pulling me against him the instant our shoes hit the pavement.

He's smooth.

And amazingly, I'm kind of okay with this ...

There's nothing wrong with allowing myself to have a good time with him. None of it means I have to sleep with him. All he asked for was a date. Nothing more, nothing less.

I breathe him in as we walk beneath a starry sky, downtown block after downtown block. Soon we're surrounded by the tail lights of taxi cabs and Lyfts, the humming and whirring of diesel buses, and the aggressive purr of locals in their luxury sports cars.

It's a symphony of sights, sounds, and smells—one I'll forever remember long after tonight, I'm sure.

The last date I was on happened at a little café on 9th Street. We drove separately. Endured an hour of stifled, forced conversation. Paid separately. Then went our separate ways. Even the drama major I dated took me on the most unimaginative, zero-effort style dates. Most of the time his idea of the perfect night together was binge-watching *Game of Thrones* while I sucked him off and he hastily returned the favor. Though I will say that one time we role-played Khal Drogo and Daenerys was kind of hot ...

But still. It wasn't a date. It never was with him.

This date is barely a couple of hours old and already it blows every other date I've ever been on completely out of the water.

"You're quiet," Talon says after another block. He squeezes my hand. "What are you thinking about?"

If I tell him, I'll be showing my hand. I'll be laying down all of my cards and giving him full advantage.

But what the hell.

Maybe Aunt Bette is right.

Maybe I should live a little.

"I'm just thinking ... that I'm surprised at how easy it is to be with you," I say.

I wait for him to say something since he's always ready with the perfect thing to say at the perfect moment, but instead it happens so fast—my back against a brick building wall, his hands in my hair, his body pressed against mine, pinning me with his uncaged desire.

His mouth claims mine, but to be fair, I'm offering it on

a freaking silver platter—his for the taking. He kisses me hard and soft, fast then slow, and through his jeans I feel the outline of his arousal. While part of me wants to resist, wants to put up a fight—the other part of me is deliciously powerless with his touch and loving every minute of it.

Someone passing behind him yells at us to get a room, but we ignore him.

"You drive me wild." Talon's lips curl into a smile against mine. "And I love every fucking minute of it."

CHAPTER 16

Talon

WE SIT in my idling car in her aunt's driveway just past midnight. I swear I blinked and the night was over. Now her hand rests reluctantly on the door handle and it's time to walk her to the door.

"You have a good time tonight?" I ask. "Better than you expected?"

Her full mouth lifts into a sleepy smile, all the confirmation I need.

I climb out of the car and trek to the passenger side, but she's already let herself out. I've never been big on the old-fashioned shit but I thought I needed to pull out all the stops tonight, take her on a date unlike any she's ever been on.

Assuming, of course.

I have no idea what kinds of dates she's been on. I only know that most guys won't take the time to plan anything remotely memorable. It just so happened that my father's namesake art exhibit fell on this weekend and I'm well aware of the fact that Irie's interests align with that. It also just so happened that the owner of Ultra is a huge PVU Tigers fanatic and all I had to do was make a phone call and he found room for us on the guest list. I wanted our date to be as intimate as it was memorable, and taking her to any old bar wasn't going to cut it.

Placing my hand on her lower back, I walk her to the door.

We stop on the front stoop of her aunt's bungalow, under the soft glow of a single outside light. Her mouth is still swollen from that kiss we had against that building on 27th Street earlier and I can still taste her on my tongue.

What I wouldn't give to take her home with me for the night.

But judging by the dreamy look in her eyes and the way her teeth bite into her ripe lower lip, I know it's only a matter of time.

Reaching for her face, I graze my fingers along her jaw before coming in for a kiss.

I leave her with something tender this time. I don't ravish her.

I need to leave her wanting more of me so when she finally caves it'll have been worth the wait—for both of us.

"Goodnight, Irie." I trail my fingertips down her arm.

"Goodnight," she says, eyes bright in the moonlight as she watches me walk away.

By the time I get back to my car, she's inside, and before I head back to my apartment, I check my phone for the first time in hours. It'd been going nuts earlier, vibrating every fucking five seconds, and finally I had to shut it off.

The instant I power it on, I find at least twenty-eight messages ... mostly from my roommates, a few of the players, and a handful of acquaintances who are convinced we're bros.

DEREK HOTCHKISS: Dude! You took Irie out tonight? Tell me you tapped that!

MATT STEVENS: Heard you bagged Irie Davenport. About f-ing time, man...

ALISON SOMERS: Who's the mystery girl? Someone posted a pic of you and some girl on a date. I thought you didn't date???

A handful of people have sent me various iPhone paparazzi style pictures of Irie and I on our date tonight. I guess some bastards have nothing better to do than concern themselves with other people's shit. Funny, I was so enamored with her all evening, I didn't even realize people were taking pics.

I toss my phone in the passenger side seat, crack the windows, tune the satellite radio to a lounge station that plays the kind of underground chill they were spinning at Ultra tonight, and then I back out of the driveway.

It's none of anyone's fucking business, and I don't need to explain myself.

Besides, if I were to start bragging about how incredible Irie is, there'll be a thousand guys beating down her door this time tomorrow. It's that influencer-generation. Everybody wants what everybody else has.

But Irie? She's mine. And I'm keeping her to my damn self.

Fifteen minutes later, I'm home.

The place is dark and lifeless—all three of my roommates were talking about hitting up some party on the west side tonight.

Trekking to my room in the back of the apartment, I peel off tonight's clothes and perch on the edge of the bed, phone in hand as I pull up my email and tap out a message.

TO: davenport.irie@pvucampusmail.edu

FROM: gold.talon@pvucampusmail.edu

SUBJECT: Best. Date. Ever. (If I do say so myself ...)

MESSAGE: Seeing as how I still don't have your phone number, I'm left with no choice but to email you so I can tell you what a fan-fucking-tastic night I had with you. Let's it again. Soon. ~Tal

CHAPTER 17

Irie

"SO WHAT YOU'RE saying is, he took you on the best date of your life and it's basically a one and done thing for you?" Brynn asks as she plops down on my bed Sunday afternoon, belly first. She cups her chin on top of her hands, examining me.

I shrug. "At the end of the day, he's still only after that one thing."

"So?"

"So ... we had a great time, but it'd be different if he was being genuine about it," I say. "Underneath it all, he's a man on a mission, and I'm not naïve enough to believe that's changed."

"Maybe you're looking at this all wrong. Maybe you should stop thinking about what he wants out of this and start thinking about what you want instead," she says. "You want to have a good time, right?"

I nod. "Who doesn't?"

"A guy like him is probably dynamite in bed." She lifts her brows and clucks her tongue. "Isn't there a part of you that wants to see what he could to do you?" She points a finger at me before I have a chance to respond. "And don't say no because I won't believe you."

I laugh. "Of course I'm curious. But that's not the point."

"Then maybe it should be."

I take a seat at my desk and crack the lid on my laptop to check my email. I've never seen Brynn so obsessed with my sex life before—then again, I'm pretty sure she thinks I was some kind of virgin when she met me because it wasn't the kind of thing I ever discussed with anyone since the events that transpired my senior year of high school.

I double-click on my inbox and tap the 'get mail' button. The screen fills with half a dozen emails, most of which are spam.

Except one.

My stomach flutters without permission as I scan his words.

Let's do it again. Soon ...

The next thing I know, I'm fighting a grin so wide it makes my cheeks ache.

"What?" Brynn asks, climbing off the bed. "What are you beaming about over there?"

Within seconds she's lurking over my shoulder, eyes scanning Talon's email.

"Oh my God. Look at you, Irie. You're blushing," she says, nudging my shoulder. "You *like* him! I knew it."

Maybe I do.

Maybe I don't.

Maybe it doesn't matter.

I close the laptop lid without responding.

It doesn't matter if I had fun last night. It doesn't matter if my ego relishes in his flattery. It doesn't matter if I want to let him kiss me again, if I want to see him again and again and again ...

It was a one date deal, and I meant what I said.

I won't date him.

I can't.

CHAPTER 18

Talon

LONGMIRE DISMISSES us five minutes early Monday morning. Irie packs up and I follow her to the hall.

"You get my email?" I ask.

"Yes." Her silky hair curtains the side of her face.

"And?"

Irie turns to me, her iridescent gaze penetrating mine. She begins to say something until some douche squeezes past and knocks me into her.

"Jesus Christ." I yell after him, "Watch your fucking step, asshole." Turning to Irie, I say, "You okay?"

"I'm fine."

A couple of girls pass by, staring and whispering. I'm sure they're looking at Irie and wondering what she has that they don't. Not that it's any of their business, but the answer is: *everything*.

"So," I say. "What are you doing this weekend?"

"Talon." She exhales, arms crossed and head tilted. "We

had a one date agreement. One date and you were going to stop."

"But you had a good time, did you not?"

"Of course I did."

"So why can't we do it again?" I ask.

A guy and girl point at us in passing the way a tourist would point at a celebrity from the top of a Hollywood tour bus. Why these people give such a shit about my personal life, I'll never understand. It's pathetic, honestly.

"Can we talk about this later?" she asks.

"When?" I ask. "You won't even give me your number."

"Thursday," she says. "We'll talk about it before we study."

"You're going to make me wait three days ..."

She peers over my shoulder, toward the exit. I know my time with her is reduced to seconds, but I'll be damned if I have to wait three whole days before discussing this with her again.

"I had a great time. You had a great time," I say. "All I'm suggesting is that we do it again."

Irie drags in a ragged, defeated breath as she adjusts the strap on her shoulder.

"I know what I said. I know I told you one date and I'd leave you alone if that's what you wanted," I say. "So tell me, Irie. Is that what you want? And I want you to think carefully before you answer. I want you to be two hundred percent sure. Because whatever you say right here, right now—"

"—yes," she blurts.

"Yes?" I ask, lips twisting into a buoyant half-smile. "As in *yes* you want to go on another date or *yes* you want me to leave you alone?"

She worries her bottom lip between her teeth, gazing up

at me through a fringe of thick lashes. "Yes, I'll go on another date with you."

Sweet Jesus.

Hooking my hand around the crook of her elbow, I pull her around the corner, to a section of hallway a little less occupied, and when I have her all to myself, I back her against the wall before claiming her cherry lips that curl against mine with the very smile she'd been fighting the past five minutes.

"I'm going to be late for class," she says a moment later, her hand pressed against my beating chest. Irie's full mouth slips into the cutest of smiles that fades in seconds, and then she's on her way.

I knew she'd come around …

CHAPTER 19

Irie

"LET THERE BE LIGHT," Aunt Bette says Thursday night as she lights two ivory-colored pillar candles on the kitchen table while Talon and I finish up our slices of delivery pizza.

They say it never rains in Southern California, but tonight is an exception. It's been pouring all day, gray skies and wet streets and air so thick with humidity your lungs begin to drown the instant you step outside. In some ways it reminds me of home, only not in a good way.

It's nothing that makes me nostalgic.

I'm not sure I could ever be nostalgic for a place like that, a place polluted with the worst kinds of memories.

I tried to call off our study plans, telling Talon we could always quiz each other over the phone, but he insisted—as per usual—that we not call off our face-to-face meeting. He's aced all of the Friday quizzes so far and he doesn't want to jinx himself.

Though if you ask me, it's just another excuse of his to milk his time with me.

After class this past Monday, he cornered me, asking me out on another date.

It was easy to ignore his email all day Sunday, easy to convince myself that I could be strong and hold firm in my decision not to take this beyond the first date—but everything changes when I'm with him.

One look at his dimpled smirk, one inhalation of his clean scent and he dismantles my heart with the skill and ease of a practiced bomb technician.

"Aren't you going to eat with us?" I ask Bette as she shuffles around the kitchen in her slippers and robe.

"Of course not. *Wheel* is on," she says. But I know her better. Bette loves her some *Wheel of Fortune*, but she's got other motives tonight. A few seconds later, she's setting up shop in her recliner, eating her pizza from a TV tray as Pat Sajak's face fills the screen on the other side of the room.

Talon and I exchanged amused chuffs as he dabs his mouth with a paper napkin. The glow of the candle flickers between us and rain beads soft on the window beside us.

As soon as we're finished, I grab my notebook and start quizzing him on the week's lecture. We're halfway finished when Aunt Bette shuffles in with her empty plate as a Norwegian cruise lines commercial plays from the next room.

"How's the studying going?" Bette asks.

"It's going ..." I say.

"You know, Irie, I was going to say, now that the two of you are dating, you should invite Talon to your cousin's wedding next month!" Aunt Bette claps her hands together.

I cannot believe she's doing this.

No, wait. Actually I can.

I never should have told her I agreed to a second date with him because now she thinks we're officially dating.

Talon's gaze snaps to mine but his expression is blank. I can imagine the last thing he wants to do is go to some stranger's wedding in BFE, Missouri.

"You should come with us," Bette says to him. "It's the weekend before spring break. We're going up Friday and coming back Sunday so you'll still get to enjoy your week off. You ever been to Missouri?"

"No, ma'am, can't say that I have," he answers, though he's still looking at me, trying to gauge my reaction in real-time. "Though I've always wanted to go."

"Liar," I mouth to him, my back to Aunt Bette.

He cracks a smile. "No, really. I think it could be fun."

"What are you doing?" I ask him, voice low.

"I don't want to invite myself along or anything," he says, "but if you need a date ..."

"Of course she needs a date," Bette says. "You know her ex-boyfriend will probably be there and last time she went home, the son of a bitch wouldn't leave her alone for two seconds."

Great.

Let's bring he-who-shall-remain-nameless into this.

Thanks a lot, Aunt Bette ...

"He's a real asshole," she says. "Personally, I can't stand the prick."

Talon tries not to laugh at Aunt Bette, hiding his face behind his napkin. And I get it. It's kind of hilarious watching a sweet, pint-sized, little old lady swear like a sailor. It took a solid year for that novelty to wear off for me.

"He could use a big guy like you to put him in his place," she says.

"Aunt Bette, I'm sorry but we're trying to study," I say.

"Ah, that's right. Got carried away there for a second," she says, giving us a wink as she shuffles back toward the living room. "Just pretend I'm not here. And I mean that. Seriously."

As soon as she's out of earshot, I apologize to Talon. "She shouldn't have put you on the spot like that. By no means would I ever expect you to go to my cousin's wedding."

"What if I want to go?"

Leaning back in my chair, I cross my arms and peer at him through the flowing candlelight that fills the space between us. "Then I'd say you're crazy. Certifiably."

"Why?" Talon shrugs. "I love meeting new people. And I bet your family would love me."

I almost choke on my spit. "My family doesn't even love themselves. They're just a bunch of perfectionistic, miserable jerks who think the only way to get the devil out of you is to handle some snakes and speak in tongues and if that doesn't work, they take you out back and beat him out of you."

He laughs.

If only I were joking.

"Seriously, you do not have to go," I say. "I don't even want to go. Only reason I am is because Bette needs my help. She can't travel on her own anymore."

"Take me with you. I'll be your buffer. I'll be your excuse when you need one. Your escape from the chaos. You can show me where you grew up, where you went to high school …" he says. "I think it'd be fun."

"It's your last spring break. Ever. I'm sure you can find something more exciting to do. Aren't your friends going somewhere? Cabo or Palm Beach or something?"

"Of course." Talon places his hand over mine. "But I'd

rather be in Missouri with you than lazing out by some pool with a bunch of drunk idiots."

I have to admit, it'd be nice having a buffer there. A reason to sneak away. A distraction.

"My aunt and uncle are going to make you stay at a hotel," I say.

"That's fine."

"They're not warm and fuzzy," I say.

He sniffs, unfazed. "Neither am I, so already we have that in common."

"I can't believe you want to do this."

His hand is still cupped over mine, the melting candle flickering between us.

"You're crazy," I say, hiding my smile behind my fingers as I shake my head at him.

Talon reaches for my hand, pulling it away before he leans in, letting his lips graze mine.

"Crazy about *you*," he says.

And then he kisses me.

Right there.

In Aunt Bette's kitchen, next to an open box of takeout pizza, paper plates, and salt and pepper shakers shaped like cacti.

The rain pelting the window outside intensifies. Back home, when it would rain this hard, most people would stay off the road. It's not safe to drive if you can't see where you're going.

Looks like he's going to be here a while.

And I think I'm okay with that.

For now.

CHAPTER 20

Talon

I SECURE a towel around my waist Saturday morning as I step out of the locker room showers in a cloud of steam.

"Dude, you've been MIA this week," Vin Chalmers says, snapping a towel at me—and missing—when I get to my locker. "What's up with that?"

"Bullshit. I've been here every day." Not that it's any of his business. "Just not at five AM anymore."

"You're screwing that weird Irie chick, right?"

My jaw flexes. *Weird?* "You want to try saying that again?"

Just because someone goes left when everyone else goes right doesn't make them *weird*.

"That Irie girl. You're screwing her," he changes his tune. "Right?"

"Fuck off, Vin," I say, not in the mood. Now that I've got Irie right where I want her, I'm not going to let anything jeopardize that, especially not nosy assholes who have no qualms about sticking their nose where it doesn't belong.

"Jesus." He flings his towel over his shoulder. A few guys on a bench a few feet down stop what they're doing and tune into our conversation. "The fuck is your problem?"

He walks away. Maybe I was a little harsh, but Irie is a sensitive subject for me. She's so much more than some girl I've been chasing the last few years, the embodiment of my failures, my weakness, and my hopes for the future.

As cliché as it sounds, Irie Davenport is my real-life dream girl.

I'll protect that any way I can, especially if it means having to make a lesson out of Vin Chalmers. He's always sticking his nose in everyone's business anyway. No one wants to fuck his loud-mouthed ass so he lives vicariously through everyone else.

I get dressed and check my phone on the way out, listening to a voice message from Ira.

"Talon, it's Ira," he says. "Why the hell haven't you signed yet? What are you waiting on, kid? The deal's not going to get any sweeter than this, so hope you're not holding out. Call me. Let me know what's going on, if there's anything I can do."

I delete the message.

I'll call him later.

I haven't signed because I haven't signed.

That's all he needs to know for now.

A few minutes later, I climb into my car and drive back to my apartment, windows down and music so loud it makes me forget about everything but *her* ...

... and what I'm going to ask her tonight.

I want her to be mine. Exclusively. Indefinitely.

I don't want to have to beg Irie for another date and

another, Saturday after Saturday. I want to be her standing weekend plans. I want to be in her life, in her schedule, in her mind ... in her body.

No more playing around.

Tonight, I'm making her mine.

CHAPTER 21

Irie

"I SIGNED THE CONTRACT," I tell Aunt Bette Saturday afternoon as I wash dishes. "It's official. Two weeks after graduation, I'll be the head of the Kira Kepner Interiors in Malibu."

Aunt Bette throws her arms around me. "I'm so proud of you. I really am. You've worked your ass off for this."

Knowing I'll be leaving her, leaving the only real home I've ever known, is a jagged little pill that doesn't want to go down all that easily.

"Are you sure you're going to be okay without me?" I ask her. I offered to bring her with me to Malibu, but she insisted she stay here. All of her friends are here, her life is here. She told me if she outlives them all, she'll join me, but until then she wants to stay put.

"I'll be fine. I think Gladys is going to move into your old room and we're going to share her assistant," Aunt Bette says with a twinkle in her eye. I've seen Gladys' assistant.

He'd make my eyes twinkle too if he were going to be waiting on me hand and foot. "Just promise you'll come back and visit."

"Of course," I tell her.

"This was more than an arrangement to me," she says. "You filled a void I never knew I had. Never wanted kids of my own, but if I'd have had a daughter, I'd have wanted her to be just like you."

She releases her hold on me and I turn away, blinking the sentimental tears away before she sees them.

I've never been good at showing emotion in front of other people.

"You're going to go out and celebrate tonight, aren't you?" she asks, taking a seat at the table.

"I have a date tonight, remember?"

"Oh, that's right! With that hunky football player. What's his name again?"

I turn to face her, chuckling. "You literally invited him to fly home with us to Lauren's wedding and you don't know his name?"

"It's something with a T ... Trent or Taron ..."

"Talon."

"Ah, yes. Like an eagle's claw," she says, rolling her eyes. "Who the hell names their kid Talon, anyway? What's the matter with John or Ricky or Tommy?"

"Same could be said about Irie ..." I remind her, though she's well aware of the fact that my mother was going through some Rastafarian phase when she was pregnant with me. The word "irie" means "good, excellent, all right," which is exactly how she felt when she held me in her arms the first time.

She was also probably high on drugs in that moment too.

"Talon's father is a famous architect. Did I tell you that?" I ask.

"No, you didn't."

"We actually studied him in school," I say.

"Seems like you're really hitting it off with this guy. Have to say, Irie, I'm pleasantly surprised."

"You and me both," I say. "Though you may have scared him off with the pizza and candles. Don't think I don't know what you were trying to pull ..."

Bette chuckles. "There's no scaring off a guy who looks at you like you hung the moon—or the stadium lights."

"I can't believe you invited him to Lauren's wedding, by the way. Totally didn't see that one coming."

She waves a limp hand. "I'm sorry, but one of us needs to keep things interesting around here. You and I both know the wedding's going to be a complete snooze fest."

"You don't think you should have asked first? They're going to freak if I just show up with some random guy."

"Let them *freak*." Bette rolls her eyes. "They *freak* all the time at church, do they not?"

I stifle a laugh. No disrespect to God or anything, but it's impossible to keep a straight face at their church when the pastor busts out the snakes and tambourines.

"And Lauren," Bette says, "one look at Talon and she's going to be green with envy. I've only met Jack a couple of times, but I've never met anyone so dreadfully dull. They make a perfect couple though. I'll give them that. They've certainly found their match."

I think back to my cousin, who's always taken her competitiveness with me to impressive levels. If I mentioned getting an A on an English test, she'd immediately mention the A+ she got in AP English the year before. If I said I went to bed early the previous night, she'd brag about how she always went to bed early and all the reasons why it made her so perfect at everything she ever did.

After a while, it became a game to me. I'd make shit up just to mess with her, and then I'd call her out on her lies in front of everyone.

She grew to hate me.

Which was probably why I'd never seen her so thrilled the day the entirety of our Iron Cross high school turned against me our senior year. It was like she'd won the lottery and a lifetime membership to Disneyland. She was straight up giddy for months after, even sneaking her way into my old circle of friends, filling the void I left with her perfect blonde bob and prissy little strut.

I shudder thinking back to that time in my life, how it seemed it would never end. It just kept going on and on, a teenage personal hell.

My stomach twists when I think about setting foot in Iron Cross again. I haven't so much as visited since they put me on a plane and shipped me out here the summer after my senior year. If it weren't for the fact that Aunt Bette really wants to go for some insane reason and can't travel alone, I'd have RSVP'd to Lauren's wedding with a drawing of a middle finger.

I dry the final dish and place it on the rack next to the sink before sliding my phone from my back pocket, checking my email out of habit.

My heart skips two beats

TO: davenport.irie@pvucampusmail.edu
FROM: gold.talon@pvucampusmail.edu
SUBJECT: Tonight
MESSAGE: Seeing as how we're technically dating

now … I think it's only fair you finally give me your number. See you @ 7. ~Tal

I wouldn't say we're technically dating, but I will say that exchanging numbers might not be the worst thing in the world at this point—if only for convenience purposes.

I fire back a quick message that contains nothing more than my phone number, and then I head to my room to start getting ready for tonight.

I have no idea how he can possibly top last weekend, but I kind of can't wait to find out …

Talon isn't at all what I expected. He's endearing and polite, attentive and generous. Part of me is pleasantly surprised. The other part of me is wishing I was right about him from the start because it'd make resisting him a walk in the park.

It would make the butterflies in my middle fly away.

I think I'm falling …

Maybe …

Sort of …

Just a little …

CHAPTER 22

Talon

I REFRESH my email for the twelfth time before I finally see it.

TO: gold.talon@pvucampusmail.edu
FROM: davenport.irie@pvucampusmail.edu
SUBJECT: Re: Tonight
MESSAGE: 555 – 0797

Wasting no time, I program her number into my phone and hit the shower. An hour later, I'm cruising across town, windows down on this uncharacteristically balmy winter day. I found a new lounge on the west side of town in this trendier neighborhood that I think she's going to like—not that she's into trendy shit, but it's definitely the kind of respectable place where you can kick off a hot date with a couple of drinks.

Fifteen minutes later, I'm pulling into Bette's driveway.

I check my reflection in the rearview, finger comb my hair into place, and make my way to the front door.

I barely knock twice when it swings open and Bette stands there in her curlers and robe, wearing a wide grin that sets off her sparkling gray eyes.

"Hey there, handsome," she teases, before calling over her shoulder, "Irie! He's here!"

I smirk. She's fucking adorable, she really is. I wish I had an Aunt Bette in my life.

"Okay, I'm ready." Irie appears from behind Bette a moment later, squeezing past in her little black shorts, fuck-me heels, and strapless top. I try not to be obvious when I drink her in from head to toe—or when my gaze settles on her juicy red pout.

Red lip gloss—does she really thinks that's going to stop me from kissing her tonight?

"You want to stare a little longer or can we get going?" she asks, giving my shoulder a soft punch with her fist.

"I'm sorry. It's just ..." I meet her gaze with a silent apology. "I'm the luckiest bastard in the world to get to take you out, that's all."

"*Staaahp*. You talked me into a second date. At this point I think you can dial down the flattery," she says as she walks down the steps and makes her way to the car, her heels clicking against the pavement with each long-legged stride.

"Not flattering you. Just being honest," I say, maneuvering around her and getting the passenger door.

Making my way to the driver's side, I catch her checking her reflection in the side mirror for two seconds—proof that she wants to look good for me ... which is also proof that she cares what I think of her ... which is also proof that she's beginning to like me.

Even if she won't admit it yet.

———

WE'RE on our second round of drinks at the Hyacinth when my filter loosens and my impatience wears off.

"I think we should date exclusively," I tell her.

She places her drink down so hard a bit of pink liquid sloshes over the rim and falls on her marble coaster.

"Whoa, whoa, whoa. Warn a girl before you drop a bombshell like that," she says. "Shouldn't we wait and see how the rest of the night goes? We're only thirty minutes into our second date. A little early to start talking all crazy." Her words are slow and relaxed and her eyes are smiling. She's making light of this, brushing it off like I'm half-kidding, half-flirting.

"Irie, I'm being serious," I say.

She twists the stem of her cocktail glass between her thumb and forefinger, the nails of which are painted the color of snow. "What's the point of labels anyway, you know?"

"I used to say the exact same thing. But now I'm thinking there's something sexy about it. So much implied in that one little word. Boyfriend. Girlfriend. Whatever. If I told someone you were my girlfriend, it'd take all of two seconds for them to know exactly how I feel about you."

"I signed a contract today," she says, taking a sip. "I'll be starting a job in Malibu two weeks after graduation."

"That's great," I say.

She laughs through her pointed nose. "You don't mean that."

"You're right." I exhale. "I mean, I'm sorry. I'm happy

for you. I am. Hell. Landing a job straight out of school is big. Congrats."

I lift my glass and clink it against the rim of hers.

"You're going to Richmond in a few months, I'm going to Malibu," she says. "I'm flattered that you want to date me exclusively, but there's really no point. We're young. We've got our whole lives ahead of us. And we both know long-distance relationships don't work. Life's already complicated enough, don't you think?"

"Can't you technically work anywhere?"

"With Kira Kepner? No. She's only based in California."

"No, I mean as a designer."

"Well, yeah, but Kira offered me my dream job and a six-figure salary. I'd be insane to walk away from that ..."

She doesn't finish her thought, but she doesn't have to. I already know what she was implying, and she isn't wrong. She'd be insane to walk away from her dream job to follow some guy she barely knows across the country so he can live his best life.

"I can't believe you'd even suggest that."

"I'm sorry." I exhale. "I didn't realize it was your dream job. You never talk about it that much ... I had no idea how much it meant to you."

Her expression softens and she's quiet for a beat. "Well, now you know."

"There has to be a way," I say, getting back on track. There always is.

Irie lifts a bare shoulder to her ear. "I don't do long-distance relationships. I don't know what else to tell you."

"Then give me the rest of the semester with you. I'd rather have that than nothing at all."

"What part of *let's just have fun and not make this complicated* did you not catch earlier?" she asks.

"We can have fun without making things complicated," I say. Our hands rest on the table and my fingers forage for hers until they become intertwined. "I don't care what comes next. I only care about right here, right now. You and me. I want to cram four years' worth of *what might have been* into this last semester. It's going to be challenging as hell, but there's nothing I love more than a good challenge."

Her full lips part, still slicked with their candy-apple shine. "You don't think you're rushing this a bit?"

"Oh, I know I am," I say. What choice do I have when it's the last quarter and the clock is ticking? "Be mine for the rest of the semester, Irie. And I'll be yours."

Her gaze drifts to the half-empty cocktail before her as she loses herself in thought for a moment, and I take the opportunity to pluck a napkin off the table and swipe it across her full lips until all traces of red are gone and it's nothing but her full lips in all of their bare glory.

Leaning in, I taste her mouth, sweet like the hibiscus flower in her drink, electric like the peppermint gum she popped in her mouth when she thought I wasn't looking earlier.

"What do you say?" I ask, voice low against her ear.

Her body rises and falls with the deepest of breaths. "Yes."

CHAPTER 23

Irie

TALON'S CHILDHOOD home makes the Vanderbilt Estate look like a backwoods vacation cabin. Okay, I'm exaggerating, but good Lord. The ornate pillars and manicured boxwoods and alabaster fountain in the driveway make simply pulling up an experience to remember. And the windows. This thing has windows for days.

He parks the BMW along the circle drive before leaning across the center console, cupping my cheek in his hand and depositing a kiss on my mouth. It's been exactly one week since he asked me to be his exclusive.

I still can't believe I said yes.

"Fair warning," he says. "They're assholes, but they're going to love you."

I was taken aback when he asked me to join him this weekend in Laguna Cove for his mom's birthday. He said she was having a small family gathering at his house and he thought it'd be a good opportunity for me to meet everyone.

If you ask me, this isn't my definition of just having fun—this is taking things to the next level. But I managed to talk myself into it by realizing I had nothing to lose by coming ... not to mention I thought it'd be neat to meet the woman who was once married to an architectural legend.

A moment later, Talon leads me to the front doors, which must stand at least thirteen or fourteen feet in height. A woman in a gray uniform-style dress greets us, letting us know everyone's outside in the rose garden.

"You grew up here?" I ask, making sure I whisper so my voice doesn't echo and bounce off the golf-leafed walls.

He slips his hand in mine. "Technically I grew up in Maritime Valley, but we moved here when I was in junior high ... after Mark had his *record* nine-figure year."

I pick up on a hint of contempt in his voice, but I don't pry. Not here. Not when we're five steps from a wall of sliding glass doors and a small gathering of Talon's family members on the other side of it.

"Look who's here!" A lithe woman with coffee-brown hair and a colorful Pucci dress rises from an iron patio chair and ambles toward us, arms stretched wide toward Talon. She wraps him in her arms like she hasn't seen him in a hundred years, and then she kisses the side of his cheek. He fights a boyish smile that disappears in under two seconds.

"Mom, this is Irie," he says. "My girlfriend. Irie, this is my mother ... Camilla."

His mom does a doubletake, giving me an obvious once over but not in any kind of rude way, more of a genuinely surprised sort of way. She takes my hand in hers, patting the top of mine as she speaks. "You said you were bringing a *friend*. I had no idea you were bringing this pretty little thing. When did you two start dating?"

"Just last week, actually," I answer.

"Well, I'll be," Camilla says, her overfilled lips arching up at the corners. "You know you're the first girl he's ever brought home."

I turn to Talon. "Really?"

His hands slide in the front pockets of his ripped jeans. "Yep."

"So, tell me, how did you two meet?" she asks, leading me to the empty chair beside her. Everything's happening so fast, I hardly have time to take in the beautiful flower-filled urns that surround us, the soft spa-like music emanating from hidden speakers, and the crash of the ocean on the shore behind us.

Talon joins us.

"We met our freshman year," he answers. "Took this long for her to give me a chance."

He winks at me.

"What? Oh, come on now," Camilla says, chuckling like she thinks he's teasing. If only she knew the truth. "Irie, would you like something to drink? Marta made the most *divine* white sangria you'll ever taste in your life. Mark, will you pour Irie a glass of the sangria, please?"

I realize now that there's a man standing behind the outdoor bar, not smiling, not saying a word. Talon said his parents were assholes ... but so far his mom is adorable. Maybe his stepdad is enough of an asshole for the two of them?

Before I forget, I reach into my bag and pull out her birthday gift. Talon insisted it wasn't necessary, that she has everything an Orange County woman could ever possibly want and then some. But I didn't want to show up empty-handed.

"This is for you," I say, handing her a small wrapped box. "Happy birthday."

Camilla places a manicured hand over her heart and looks at me with tenderness in her eyes. "Aren't you just the sweetest thing?"

A moment later, she unwraps the gift and examines the small marble ring box. It's the kind of item that looks perfect staged on a guest room nightstand or alongside a bathroom sink. Carrera marble goes with just about anything, and it's timeless and elegant.

I figured with her interior design background, she'd appreciate such a classic, versatile accessory.

"This is gorgeous, Irie, thank you so much," she says, running her fingertips along the smooth edges. "I know exactly where I'm going to put this."

Placing it aside with care, she leans over and gives me another hug. Her perfume is distinct and overwhelming yet lovely—much like her home.

A few seconds later, a soft-bellied, bald-headed man shuffles across the patio to offer me a glass of white sangria accented with various floating fruits.

"Irie, this is Mark," Talon says. "My stepdad."

"Wonderful to meet you," I say as we shake hands.

"Likewise," He says, monotone, his attention veering toward Talon. He makes a face, somewhere between a sneer and a wince. And then it's gone. Maybe I imagined it?

"Irie's an interior design major," Talon says to his mom.

"Oh, you're *kidding*." She swats her hand against my knee, her eyes sparkling.

"Talon told me you used to design," I say.

"I sure did." There's life in her effervescent voice. "That's how I met Talon's father actually. He was an architect and we met at this conference in Pacific Heights."

"I'm very familiar with his work," I say. "Talon actually

took us to the Gold-Harris exhibit a couple of weekends ago. Amazing, *amazing* work."

As I geek out with his mother, Talon sits back in silence, his stare weighty and obvious.

"Talon." Mark takes a seat next to him, slapping his knee. "How's the new training schedule? Still hitting the gym every day?"

Talon's chest rises and falls and his lips flatten. "You ask me that every single time you see me."

"Oh, come on. Someone's gotta stay on top of you." Mark sniffs, like he's teasing. Talon gives him a thousand-yard stare. "I only ask because I care."

I try to pay attention to what Camilla's saying—something about this "painted lady" she was hired to renovate in San Francisco when she was fresh out of design school—but I'm distracted by the tense energy I'm picking up on from Talon, a vibe that only seemed noticeable the instant Mark sat down.

I take a sip of the white sangria, saccharine sweet with just enough of a kick to it, and nod along to what she's saying until the sliding door behind her opens and a teenage girl with wavy blonde hair down to her lower back steps out, cell phone in hand.

"Hadley," Camilla says. "How was practice?" She turns to me. "Hadley's on the competitive dance squad at her school. Last year they went to state. Fingers crossed we take home the big trophy this year."

I'm beginning to sense a pattern with these people—the emphasis on winning and accolades and bragging rights. And knowing what I know about Talon, it makes perfect sense.

Hadley takes a seat in a chair at the far end of the table,

nose buried in her phone. She's here but she isn't. She's simply making an appearance.

"Hadley, have you met your brother's girlfriend?" Camilla asks. "Come say hi to Irie."

The blonde glances up from her phone for half of a second before returning her attention to her screen and staying planted.

"Teenagers," Mark says with a huff. Funny he seems adamant about staying on top of Talon's workout schedule yet he doesn't give a damn about his daughter's disrespect.

"Where's Kelsey?" Camilla asks. "I should go find her. Lucille should be bringing dinner out any minute. Would you all excuse me for a moment?"

With that, Camilla disappears into the house, her overflowing wine glass in hand, and Mark pushes himself to a standing, heading to the outdoor bar to refill his crystal tumbler with cognac he pours from a leather-wrapped bottle.

"I want to see your room," I say. "I want to see where teenage Talon got his start."

"It's boring."

"I doubt that."

"And it looks nothing like it did when I was younger. I think it's on Mom's fifth iteration ..."

"Come on ..."

He flashes an amused smirk and heads in. I follow. It seems like we're walking forever when we finally reach a curved staircase in the back of the house. We make our way to the top, hand in hand, before he leads me down a dark hallway, stopping at the last door on the right.

"All right. This is it," he says. "This is my childhood bedroom."

He swings the door open, and we're met with a small

gush of air that smells like a mix between organic cleaning spray and the salty spray of the Pacific ocean.

The walls are covered in navy wallpaper with the tiniest hint of a pattern, and the furniture is polished white oak. It's equal parts coastal and castle—a difficult blend if I do say so myself—but somehow it works.

A king-sized bed is centered against one wall, anchored with oversized nightstands and gold-toned lamps, and a row of windows along the far wall showcases the stunning ocean view.

"Can't imagine what it must have been like growing up with views like this," I say, heading to the windows. "Falling asleep at night to the sound of real ocean waves."

"I was never really home all that much," he says. "Between school and training and games, I was only really here to sleep and by then, I'd be so exhausted I'd fall asleep with my cleats on half the time."

"Well that's a shame," I say. He's standing beside me now, his body heat subtle but his presence heavy.

"Yeah," he says.

"Your stepdad," I begin to say.

"What about him?"

"Is he always so ... gruff? If I didn't know any better, I'd think he's annoyed that I'm here."

Talon squints. "He probably is."

"Really? Why?"

"Don't take it personally," he says. "It's not about you. It's about football. It's always about football with him. I'm sure he thinks you're going to be a distraction to my workout schedule or some bullshit like that."

From the corner of my eye, I spot an oversized glass case filled to the brim with trophies, awards, medals, and framed photos. I'm not sure how I missed this when we walked in because now that I see it, I can't take my eyes off it. The presentation is quite ... ostentatious.

He follows my attention and exhales. "That is all my mother's doing. For the record, I would never enshrine my accomplishments."

"I think it's cute," I say, making my way over. "A little over the top, but it paints a pretty vivid picture of who you are."

He clears his throat. "Let me know when you want to head back down."

I turn to him, almost laughing. "Does this make you uncomfortable?"

I can't imagine Mr. Big Ego wanting to shy away from the limelight when all he's ever done is shine, but now that I look at him, I realize his hands are on his hips and his jaw is set and nothing about him looks like he wants to be in here, re-living his glory days.

"Are you okay?" I ask.

"What? Yeah," he says, frowning. "Just hungry."

"Liar." I study him closer. "What's going on?"

Talon's rounded shoulders lift. "I just don't like looking at any of this shit."

"This shit?" I repeat. "Talon, this is your life's work. These are your accomplishments. You should be proud to show these off."

"Yeah, well, I'm not, so—"

I'm beyond confused. "Guess I never took you for a humble guy."

"You and everyone else." His words are chilled, his delivery distant.

"Is this a sensitive subject for you?" I ask, pointing to the overflowing case.

His brows lift and he stares through me for a sec, his

hands still firm on his hips. It almost seems like he has something to say, something to get off his chest, but the words are stuck inside him.

"You're acting weird ..."

"I just ... this case represents everything I hate," he says.

"Wait. *What?*"

Talon pinches the bridge of his nose before striding to his bed and taking a seat on the edge. His body is folded over, elbows on his knees, and he releases a heavy breath.

"I've never said that before," he says.

I take the spot beside him, resting my hand on his back in a silent show to let him know I'm here for him.

Glancing up at the case on the other side of the room, his body stiffens. "I hate the game, Irie."

I'm digging deep for the right thing to say in this moment, but I'm coming up empty-handed.

"Dinner's ready," a young voice interrupts us, and we turn toward the door. A petite girl with straight dark hair leans against the jamb. "They told me to come get you guys."

"Thanks, Kels," Talon says, climbing up from the bed. He reaches for my hand and leads me out of the room, but all I can think about is that bombshell he just dropped.

I never would have seen that coming in a million years.

He always seemed so sure of himself, so confident in his talent and his goals and ambitions, but was it all for show? All for nothing? And what does it say about a man who can work so hard for so long, obsessively chasing after a single objective ... only to have a change of heart and throw it all away?

CHAPTER 24

Talon

I WAKE to the smell of bacon wafting from the kitchen Sunday morning. Reaching over, I find the spot beside me cold and vacant. Flinging the covers off, I head to the bathroom to clean up.

We left my parents' house last night and came back to my place to chill for a bit. She talked me into watching the cheesiest show she could possibly find on Netflix. We were one and a half episodes in when out of nowhere, she climbed into my lap, threw her arms around my shoulders, and crushed her petal soft lips against mine.

She kissed me hard and recklessly, zero abandon, and the way things were headed, I thought for sure last night was going to be the night, but she wasted no time pumping the brakes the second I slid my hand up her shirt.

Regardless of that setback, I convinced her to stay the night ...

I guess you could say we've slept together now—even if we were fully clothed.

I find Irie in the kitchen, along with two of my roommates who are perched on counter stools waiting for their breakfast like a couple of begging mutts.

"No, they never should have traded Voxley," Irie says, standing over a pan of sizzling bacon in nothing but one of my jersey-thin t-shirts. "And I say that as a retired Chiefs fan."

"Wrong," Carter shoots back. "I'm sorry, but you're wrong. Voxley's been worthless ever since he tore his ACL two seasons ago. Never been the same. Dude needs to hang it up."

"What?" She turns to shoot him a dirty look. "He scored more touchdowns last season than he did in the two seasons before that combined."

"Look who's up," Rylan interrupts their argument when he sees me. "Morning, angel face. Sleep well?"

He's wearing a shit-eating grin and I'm positive he thinks I fucked Irie last night, but it's none of his fucking business so whatever.

"You didn't have to do this," I tell Irie as she plates a few slices of bacon. I slip my hands around her waist from behind, leaning down to kiss her neck. "These guys might talk football like morons, but they're perfectly capable of making their own breakfast."

She smiles. "It's fine. I was up. And I was starving. Rylan's the one who went the store to get everything."

"Jesus. What time is it?" I check the clock on the microwave. It's half past nine. I don't remember the last time I slept in this late, but I must have needed it. In fact, I don't remember the last time I slept this hard. Something about having Irie beside me, lying in my arms, put me out like a light last night, despite the freight train of thoughts clouding my head.

Ever since the conversation we had over the display case at my mom's house yesterday, I can't stop thinking about what I said.

I mean, I've felt that way for years ... but saying it out loud made it real.

Irie casually tried to bring it up last night between episodes of *Jane the Virgin* or whatever the hell she had us watching, but I brushed it off every time.

I'm not ready to talk about it.

Talking about it means making a decision—a decision I've been avoiding for weeks now.

I still haven't signed the Richmond contract.

And honestly ... I don't know that I will.

CHAPTER 25

Irie

"A LOT of girls hate you right now."

I peer across the table in my lighting class Monday morning and find a girl who's never said more than three words to me all semester.

"I'm sorry, what?" I ask.

"You're dating Talon Gold, right?" she asks. "A lot of girls hate you. That, or they want to be you. You're pretty much the most infamous name on campus right now. I think someone even started a hashtag about you."

I roll my eyes and attempt to ignore the girls at the table behind us, listening intently to our conversation.

"What's your secret?" she asks. "How'd you get the one guy no one's ever been able to get?"

Without hesitation, I say, "He has a type."

"Which is?" She lifts a micro-bladed eyebrow, chewing on the end of her pencil with pillow-sized Kylie Jenner lips.

"He likes girls with tact," I say. "I think he also has a

thing for basic human decency. Oh, and self-respect. He's pretty into that."

She wrinkles her perfect nose and scoffs before turning away, and I angle myself to hide the humor trying to display itself across my lips. Maybe I came off a little harsh, but I know what she was saying underneath all of those questions.

She thinks he can do better than me.

She thinks he'd be better suited for someone like her.

I had "friends" like that back in high school—ones who'd make underhanded remarks disguised as innocent questions—and I ate them for breakfast.

Our professor excuses himself to take a phone call, and I use it as a chance to check my messages.

Sure enough, Talon texted me within the last twenty minutes.

TALON: My place tonight … seven.

I fire off a quick "if you insist" along with a winking emoji and put my phone away.

My stomach is a cage of frenzied butterflies and my head is all kinds of distracted and my lips burn in anticipation of seeing him again. We've been "dating" almost a month now and this still happens every time I think about him.

Every. Damn. Time.

He wasn't wrong when he said we could have fun together, but every part of me knows that come May, things are going to get one-hundred-and-one kinds of complicated.

CHAPTER 26

Talon

THEY SAY time flies when you're having fun and it just might be the truest words ever spoken, cliché or otherwise.

In one week, we leave for Irie's cousin's wedding in Missouri.

In two weeks, my offer from Richmond expires, which means they'll be allowed to make a new offer, one that will undoubtedly be less sweet than the first.

Music plays low from a speaker on my desk as Irie and I are sprawled across my bed on a random Thursday night.

We were supposed to be studying, but neither of us are feeling focused on anything other than each other tonight.

"It's getting late," she says, her leg intertwined with mine as I twist her soft hair in my fingers. Hozier's From Eden plays in the background, and her body is warm against me.

"Stay."

She gazes up at me through sleepy eyes, her lips pink and swollen from two solid hours of kissing me tonight.

"I can't," she says. "I've been staying over a lot lately, and that's not fair to Aunt Bette."

"Has she said something?"

"No. She hasn't. And she won't. But still. It's not right."

I stroke my hand against the side of her pretty face. I always hate when she leaves. Everything feels empty and hollow, lifeless. It's like a piece of me is missing. She's my phantom limb.

"Why are you looking at me like that?" she asks, sitting up and tucking one leg halfway beneath her.

"You think you'll miss this?" I ask.

We've been so focused on having fun this past month that we've intentionally side-stepped the inevitable—life after graduation.

"What kind of question is that?"

"Just answer."

She rolls her eyes, pretending to be annoyed. "Obviously."

"What if I never find anyone like you again?" I ask. "What we go our separate ways and I never find someone who drives me half as wild as you do?"

"I don't know why you're bringing this up right now," she says. "We went into this knowing we wouldn't have a future, remember?"

"A couple years ago, there was this volunteer board at the Memorial Union," I say. "I walked past it probably half a dozen times before I actually stopped and looked at it. Irie, your name was on every last sign-up sheet."

She shrugs. "Just doing my part."

"Where am I going to find another girl as selfless as you? As giving? I mean, you live with your eighty-year-old aunt taking care of her instead of living in some campus apartment with a bunch of friends, getting that true college experience," I continue. "And don't even get me started on the way you hold your own when other girls give you shit. You are *everything*, Irie. Inside and out."

"Everything? No one's ever called me that before."

"You're the real deal," I say. "And I know that if we walk away from this, I'm never going to find anyone half as real as you."

Irie slides off the bed and begins to gather her things from around the room—shoes, bag, phone, and when she's dressed and ready to dash out the door, she turns to me and hesitates.

"I think we're moving way too fast," she says. "And I think you're overthinking this."

"What are you trying to say?"

"That we shouldn't get ahead of ourselves or make rash decisions because we're afraid. The future is terrifying. There's never a right decision when it comes to anything."

"I disagree."

"Just ... let's have fun." Her eyes soften. "I like this ... being with you. I don't want to ruin it. I don't want to complicate it. You promised ..."

She's right.

I did.

Irie slides her hand in mine and I kiss the top, her skin cashmere-soft against my mouth.

"Goodnight, gorgeous," I say.

She smiles, lowering her swollen lips to mine one last time for the night. "See you tomorrow."

With that she's gone.

I lie in bed, staring at the ceiling, waiting for the emptiness to sink into my bones as I contemplate my future.

Sliding my hands behind my head, I drag in a heavy breath and close my eyes, imagining a life without her ... only it's depressing as fuck. The second I sign that contract and move out east, I'm going to be surrounded by opportunists, fame-chasers and plastic women who aspire to be nothing more than a baller's wife.

The creak of the door pulls me out of my silent pity party, and I sit up in bed, peering across the room to a familiar shadow standing in the doorway.

"I thought you left," I say to her.

She closes the door behind her, dropping her bag near my desk and sliding out of her shoes. "I called Aunt Bette. She doesn't need me tonight."

Irie tears off her clothes, stripping down to her bra and panties, and she helps herself to a t-shirt from my top drawer. I love how comfortable she is around me now, and I love it even more when she makes herself at home with me. A second later, she's crawling into bed with me, curling under my arm and breathing me in.

A moment ago I was tired, mentally exhausted from the heaviness of the decision weighing on me, anchored by the uncertainty of what comes after graduation, bothered by knowing a life without Irie isn't any kind of life that interests me.

And now here she is, back in my arms again, sending me high as a fucking kite.

Irie's my drug of choice, I'm woefully addicted, and I've just taken another hit.

I press a kiss into the top of her strawberry-scented head and close my eyes.

I could live in this moment forever.

CHAPTER 27

Irie

TALON IS awake before the sun comes up Friday morning, trying to quietly get his gear together for his morning workout. I stir, shifting beneath his heavy blankets before rolling to my side and watching him.

"Didn't mean to wake you," he says, shoving a small towel into his gym bag.

"It's fine." I sit up, climbing out of bed and gathering my things. "I'll walk out with you."

I change into last night's clothes and head to his bathroom to freshen up. A second later we're in the hallway of his apartment, locking up behind us before making our way to the parking lot.

Aunt Bette's been letting me drive her Crown Victoria lately. She thought it was ridiculous that it took me almost four years to even so much as ask to borrow it for personal use, but I never wanted her to think I was taking advantage of her.

Plus this thing is ancient. If it breaks down on my watch, I won't have the funds to pay for any repairs.

Talon takes my hand in his as we walk to the parking lot, where our cars are parked side by side—his shiny black Beemer and Aunt Bette's fabulous maroon Ford that's almost as old as I am.

"What's on your window?" he asks as we get closer.

"What do you mean?" I squint through the early morning darkness and scan Aunt Bette's car.

And then I see it.

The word "SLUT" dragged across the driver's side glass in red lipstick.

Original ...

"The fuck is wrong with people?" Talon throws his gym bag on the ground before rifling through it to grab his workout towel. A second later he's trying to wipe the glass clean, but he's only making it worse. The entire thing is smeared in red. "I'll be back. I'm going to grab some Windex or something. This is bullshit, Irie. I'm sorry."

In an instant, I'm taken back to a nearly identical incident my senior year at Iron Cross High. It's a moment that's stayed with me for years, despite my best efforts to erase it from my memory.

Talon disappears inside, which gives me time to fight off the wave of tears that begin to cloud my vision.

I don't want him to see this side of me.

I don't want to have to explain something he couldn't possibly begin to understand.

CHAPTER 28

Talon

I TOSS an extra pair of jeans in my suitcase and zip it shut. Tomorrow I'll be boarding a plane with Irie and Bette to Missouri for her cousin's wedding. If I'm being honest, Missouri isn't exactly on my bucket list, but I'm looking forward to a weekend away with her, a change of scenery, a glimpse of what life could be like outside the PVU bubble we know all too well.

"Dude." Rylan bursts through my door, his phone in hand. "Why didn't you tell me Irie used to be a friggin' cheerleader?"

"The hell are you talking about? Let me see." Pretty sure she would have mentioned something like that to me by now.

Rylan hands me his phone, where it appears he's Googled "Irie Davenport." If it were any other asshole, I'd clock him for it because my girlfriend is none of his damn business, but I've known Rylan since our sophomore year and he's always had a peculiar obsession with Googling everybody—it's never anything personal, it's just something he does because he's a giant fucking weirdo.

I scroll through the first image on the screen and stop on the second I recognize an all-too-familiar face. Pinching to zoom in, it takes all of a single second to confirm that it is, indeed, my girlfriend dressed in a full cheerleader's uniform, complete with a sky-high ponytail tied with a glossy red ribbon. Her hands are at her hips, fists full of red and black pom-poms, and she's grinning wide as she stands front and center before her squad.

The caption below says, "Cheer squad captain Irie Davenport does her part to lead the Iron Cross Rams to a homecoming victory."

"Huh." I hand Ryland his phone.

I can only assume there are a million other things I've yet to learn about her.

A weekend in her hometown should help fill in some of those blanks.

CHAPTER 29

Irie

"TAKE A RIGHT UP HERE," I point up ahead as Talon brings the Nissan we rented to a slow crawl just short of my aunt and uncle's driveway. "It's the white house at the end of the street."

The flight went smoothly. Aunt Bette downed two glasses of cheap chardonnay at an airport bar before we boarded, Talon zoned out with headphones in his ears, and I read a paperback I grabbed from a gift shop. There wasn't an ounce of turbulence or so much as a minute of a delay and yet I've been tense all afternoon.

My head throbs and my stomach churns.

Coming home—if I can even call it that—is something I've been dreading ever since Lauren and Jack sent their save-the-dates last fall and Bette RSVP'd the two of us.

Talon pulls into my aunt and uncle's driveway, parking off to the side. Judging by the number of unfamiliar vehicles lining the street, I'd say they're in the midst of doing some pre-wedding entertaining, which is probably a good thing. I just want to show up, make my appearance, and get the hell out of here. The fewer exchanges the better.

He kills the engine and climbs out to grab our luggage from the trunk as I help Bette out of the backseat. We're all halfway up the front walk when the door swings open and Lauren comes dashing out, a vision in a white sheath dress, her hair an icier shade of blonde than the last time I saw her.

She wraps her arms around Aunt Bette, making a show of their reunion despite the fact that Bette has never been all that fond of Lauren nor have they ever been close. But Bette plays along, hugging Lauren back and telling her how beautiful she looks.

Lauren glides her palm down the side of her head before tucking her hair behind one ear and feigning a humble thank you.

"Aunt Bette, so glad you're here," Aunt Elizabeth steps out from inside, arms wide open as she comes toward us. Her smile and embrace are reserved only for Bette, which is fine with me, but it doesn't make this moment any less awkward or uncomfortable for half of us.

"Irie," Elizabeth says, turning to me and clasping her wiry hands tight in front of her narrow hips. "Did you have a nice flight?"

"We did," I say.

Her eyes move from mine to Talon and back, her lips puckered tight. "Well, aren't you going to introduce us to your friend? I had no idea you were bringing a guest. I hope he was able to find accommodations at the Quality Inn. I know most of the good hotels are booked with wedding guests ..."

"This is Talon," I say. "My boyfriend. Talon, this is my aunt, Elizabeth."

Talon extends his hand. "Wonderful to meet you, Elizabeth. And don't worry about me. I was able to find a suite at the Hilton in Peony Falls."

Aunt Liz's dusty blue eyes flash for a second. There's nothing more this woman hates than being one-upped, and everyone knows Peony Falls is a giant step and a half up from anything Iron Cross could ever offer a visitor.

"Well, then," Liz says. "Why don't you all come in? We just got back from the rehearsal dinner. Having a small gathering for ... *close* friends and family." We head inside like ducks in a row. "Oh, and Irie, I wasn't able to get a hold of your mother, and I tried everything. I'm so sorry. I wasn't sure if you were hoping to see her or not, but I wanted to let you know."

"Did you try courier pigeon-ing the invite?" Talon asks. I told him on our first date that she lives on a technology-free commune. His dig is brilliant.

My aunt shoots him a dirty look before turning away and opting to ignore him.

I jab him in the ribs.

I should have warned him about Aunt Liz's non-existent sense of humor.

At least now he knows.

"So this is where you grew up?" he asks as we stop in the foyer. He leans down to examine the vast array of Lauren's photos that litter the marble console table against the wall. "Why aren't there any pictures of you?"

I chuff. "Because they're probably trying to erase those years from their memory."

"Why would they want to do that?"

"Because I was their worst nightmare."

He begins to say something, probably wanting me to

elaborate, when Uncle Michael rounds the corner, hands on his hips.

"Irie," he says. "Good to see you."

He doesn't mean it.

That's the thing about people like him. They say and do things they never mean all of the time because they think it makes them look better. They're always covering up their ugly souls with good deeds.

I never asked for them to take me in.

They wanted to look like saints to their congregation, like pillars to their community. Not to mention, Aunt Elizabeth always wanted more children but after Lauren, it just never happened for them. I think she had visions of dressing us like twins and showing off her beautiful, perfect china doll daughters to all of her friends at the Iron Cross Country Club.

Only none of that happened.

Lauren and I fought like, well, siblings.

And I was never the sweet, angelic niece she envisioned.

I was opinionated and sardonic and wise beyond my years—a trait thrust upon me from years of living on a commune where curfews and structure were never a thing and autonomy began by age five.

She wanted so badly to shape me into the person she wanted me to be.

Unfortunately that only worked with Lauren, who came equipped with a born-to-please-gene from birth.

"And who's your friend?" Uncle Michael says.

"This is my boyfriend," I say, swallowing the lump in my throat, one that takes me back to my senior year. "Talon, this is my uncle Michael."

They shake hands, Michael making an obvious attempt to size him up despite the fact that Talon towers over him.

"Dad, come on, we're waiting for you," Lauren says from the doorway. She doesn't so much as give me a simple greeting. "Oh, my goodness, Aunt Bette!"

She wraps her arms around Bette's shoulders, squeezing tight as if to make it look like they have such a close, wonderful bond even though we all know the truth.

"Thank you so much for coming," she says before letting her go and turning to me. "Irie."

"Lauren," I say without missing a beat.

"I'm surprised you're able to miss class to come here," she says. "I hate the idea of you falling behind just to come to my wedding..."

"It's spring break. And I wouldn't miss this for the world," I say with a faux smile that shuts her up. I'm perfectly capable of taking the high road, even if she isn't.

Her gaze travels to Talon next, and she inhales a sharp breath, her eyes widening before averting.

I know that look.

She finds him attractive...

"Lauren, this is my boyfriend, Talon," I say, hooking my arm into his and splaying my other hand across his steely chest.

Lauren clears her throat, too nervous in his presence to utter a single respectable response.

"Come on, Dad." Lauren straightens her shoulders, suddenly pretending like we're not there anymore. "They need you in the next room."

I don't know what they could possibly need him for right now. It's not like they're cutting a cake or lighting fireworks. I imagine she's jealous that his attention isn't solely on her tonight.

Sometimes I think he wanted to be a father figure to me.

Other times I think he felt guilty, like he was abandoning his own daughter if he gave me too much of his time or energy. Regardless, it's in the past now.

I don't need a father figure anymore and I don't need him.

"Talon, if you wouldn't mind taking those bags to the guest room for us, that'd be great," Uncle Michael says, speaking to him but looking at me. "Come join us in the family room when you're done."

"Of course," Talon says.

As soon as my uncle leaves, I slide my arm into his and lead him down the hallway, to the main floor guest suite that was once my teenage bedroom. I walk ahead when we get closer, grabbing the door for him.

It's been almost four years since I set foot in here, but if I'm lucky, Liz has done a full remodel and the place will hardly be recognizable.

But the second I flip the light switch, my hopes are dashed.

The place is almost exactly the way I left it, right down to the track ribbons hanging on a robe hook on the back of the closet door and the bulletin board on the wall overflowing with photos of me partaking in all those extracurriculars Liz and Michael pushed on me to keep me busy and out of trouble.

It almost worked.

Until I met Trey McAvoy.

Talon leaves the suitcases by the bed before making his way to the bulletin board, examining the pictures.

"When were you going to tell me you were a cheerleader?" he asks.

"Oh, I'm sorry. Did I leave that out?" I ask, batting my lashes. "Silly me."

"Just seems odd given the fact that I play football."

"I don't bring it up because it's ancient history. It's not a part of me anymore," I say. "It was a thing I did for a few years when I was obsessed with fitting in, dying for people to like me. That girl," I point to a picture of me in my cheerleading uniform, "cared more about what other people thought of her than what she thought of herself. She equated being used with being loved. *That* girl ... that perky little *cheerleader* ... no longer exists."

"There you are." Aunt Liz clears her throat from the doorway behind us. "I was wondering where you two were hiding. Why don't you come join us in the family room for mocktails and appetizers?"

She toys with the gold cross pendant around her neck, her attentive gawk passing between us, lingering on me after a bit as if to say, "You know the rules."

And I do.

I'm not allowed to be alone with "boys" in their home.

I swear she looks at me and still sees that misguided teenager, the one who pushed her buttons because all she ever wanted was proof that she was loved.

Turns out she never was. Not by them anyway.

And looking back, it explains so much.

CHAPTER 30

Talon

I TAKE a drink from a mocktail-filled paper cup and peruse my surroundings. Irie's aunt and uncle's place is neat and tidy but also sparse and bland, night and day from the coastal-venetian-hybrid palace I grew up in. And so far the only evidence that Irie so much as lived here—other than the bulletin board in the guest room—is a single 5x8 framed photo on a coffee table. From the looks of it, it was taken at some gargantuan family reunion where they cram all seventy-six attendees into one shot. If she weren't in the front row with the rest of the kids, I wouldn't have noticed her.

"You doing okay?" Irie asks, placing her hand softly on top of my thigh.

"Of course."

She sips from her cup, watching everyone around us socialize. So far only a handful of people have acknowledged her. Either she's the bona fide black sheep of the family or she's related to nothing but assholes.

"Irie, hi." Her cousin, Lauren, the prissiest thing this side of the Mississippi, sidles up beside us, sweeping her hands beneath her skirt before she takes a seat. Clearing her throat, she crosses her legs at the ankle. "I just thought you should know that Trey McAvoy is going to be at the wedding so please ... behave yourself. No drama."

Irie blinks once before turning still as a statue. "Why would you invite him?"

Lauren sniffs. "He works with Jack. They're good friends now. Geez, Irie, it's not about you all the time."

With that, Lauren shuffles off and I turn to my girlfriend, who is almost white as a ghost. I don't know who this fucking Trey McAvoy is, but obviously the mere mention of him is upsetting.

"Hey." I take her hand, giving it a squeeze. "What was that about?"

She shakes her head, trying to snap out of it, and then she places her drink on a nearby coaster. Her hands rake up and down her thighs, nothing but nervous energy, and then she rises, pacing the small corner of the family room we occupy.

"Irie." I stand. Something's wrong. "You want to get some air? Let's go outside."

She's barely paying attention to me, so I take her by the arm and lead her to the back door—only when we get there, I realize the patio is filled with guests.

"Let's go out front," I say, taking her to the foyer.

We step into our shoes and head out the door, and before I have a chance to say something she's halfway across the front lawn, headed for the sidewalk, arms hugging her sides.

"Irie, wait up." I jog to catch up with her. "You going to talk to me or what? You're kind of freaking me out here."

It's starting to get dark now, nothing but street lights and a dusky blue sky illuminating our way.

"Yeah, just ... give me a second," she finally speaks, her voice broken. After a block, I manage to get a better look at her and I realize she's crying. Or she was. Her cheeks are damp and rosy, her eyes glassy.

I think back to that day almost two months ago when I asked her who put that fucking wall around her heart.

Pretty sure I have my answer.

Up ahead, a massive brick building comes into focus, and a white sign out front says IRON CROSS HIGH SCHOOL. We keep striding along, Irie on a mission and me waiting with bated breath to find out what the hell this is all about, and within minutes we arrive outside an empty parking lot and the high school football stadium.

Everything is dark and empty, unoccupied and ominous, and I'm completely caught off guard when Irie heads in that direction.

Without saying a word or asking her why, I follow behind as she manages to find an unlocked portion of the fencing and then proceeds to make her way to the field. A moment later, she stops at the thirty-yard line and lowers herself to the ground.

"You going to tell me what's going on?" I ask, taking a seat beside her.

She drags in a jagged breath, nodding. Her posture is small, like she's pulling herself into some protective shell, so I take her by the arm and guide her into my lap so I can hold her.

I want her to know she doesn't have to protect herself when she's around me.

She doesn't need to make herself small.

"I'm sorry," she says, wiping a small tear from the corner of her eye and half-laughing at herself. "I'm not normally this theatrical ... about anything ... it's just ... Lauren *knew*." Her lower lip trembles. "She knew and she invited him anyway."

"Knew what?"

"About Trey," she says. Her pretty eyes squeeze tight for a second, and I brush a strand of hair from her forehead. "I've never talked about this with anyone before."

My heart stops in my chest, bracing itself to break with what she's about to tell me.

"Trey was my high school boyfriend," she begins, eyes averted. "We were together pretty much all four years and obviously he was my first ... everything." She pauses. "We were your typical small-town cheerleader-quarterback high school sweethearts ... until our senior year." Irie presses her lips flat. "We were talking one night and he confessed to me that he thought it'd be hot if we had a four-way with him and two of his friends. And honestly, I was willing to try just about anything back then because it was all so new and exciting and there was that rush I got from sneaking around and doing things behind my aunt and uncle's backs. You know ... typical teenager stuff." She rolls her eyes. "Anyway, I told him yes. I wanted to do the three-way. I thought it'd be hot and fun and something new to try. So a week later, he gets a hotel room. I tell my aunt and uncle I'm staying the night with a friend and we meet up with two of his friends from the team."

My stomach is leaden and my jaw clenches.

I know where this is going.

"One of them brought a bottle of vodka, the other

brought a box of condoms ..." her voice grows quieter. "And we had ourselves a time."

I study her face, all the conflicting micro-expressions flicking through her eyes and across her lips all at the same time.

"For the record," she says. "Everything was consensual and I had a great time. I'd never felt so ... desired ... before. And for a girl who'd never felt like anyone wanted her—it was kind of a big deal for me. Granted, I know now that I was being used, but at the time, it didn't matter. They were all over me, like they couldn't get enough, and I loved every minute of it." Irie pulls in a long breath of chilly March air. "Everything was fine until the following Monday at school."

"What happened?"

"I knew something was off when I showed up and someone had written SLUT across my locker in red lipstick," she says, eyes rolling. "And then there were the whispers. The staring, the pointing. It wasn't until lunchtime that someone finally pulled me aside and showed me the pictures that were circulating."

"My God."

"Apparently one of them had snapped a few extremely revealing photos of our night together." She shakes her head. "I must have been too drunk to notice at the time."

"You can't blame yourself for that."

"I confronted Trey about it as soon as I could," I say. "I thought surely he'd be just as upset as me and I needed someone in my corner. He was the most popular guy in school and I knew he could call off the wolves ... only instead of coming to my defense, he slut shamed me in front of everyone. He told me we were over, that I was dirty and I disgusted him."

My vision flashes red. "I'm going to kill him when I see him tomorrow. I'm going to fucking *murder* him."

She manages to snicker, like she thinks I'm kidding.

I'm not.

"Word got back to my aunt and uncle," she says. "My aunt was our high school chorus teacher and my uncle was the vice principal of the junior high. They even saw some of the photos ..."

Irie buries her face in her hands.

"It was public humiliation beyond anything you could ever imagine—and at home it was nonstop shaming," she says. "They made me go to counseling with their pastor three nights a week and then they sent me to some church-sponsored reform camp for eight weeks. I almost didn't graduate from high school because I'd fallen behind from being gone so long."

"Bastards."

"My uncle couldn't look me in the eyes for months ... my aunt played the victim card, taking it personally and obsessing over how it reflected on her. Lauren ... Lauren relished every minute of it. She loved watching my fall from grace, loved watching me become the social outcast and taking my place in my group of friends."

"Sounds like a fucking nightmare. Do you even realize how strong you are for setting foot back here again?"

"I'm only doing it for Aunt Bette."

"I know, but still." I cup the side of her face, swiping away a half-dried tear with my thumb. "Your high school boyfriend can eat a bag of fucking dicks and your family are assholes ... but you, Irie? You won."

She sniffs. "It's not about winning ..."

"Oh, but it is. You got out of here. They kicked you and you got back up. You left this sad sack town behind, you moved forward with your life while they're all still here swimming in the same disgusting waters, convincing themselves they're better than everyone else because no one's ever aired their dirty laundry."

"I don't want to talk about this anymore," she says. "I just ... I had to vent for a second. Lauren had me all worked up ..."

"Of course," I say, kissing her ice-cold lips. We lie back on the turf, and I pull her close against me, doing my best to keep her warm. I don't want to make her go back there with all those self-serving bastards, not yet.

Plus I love when it's just us—no matter where we are.

"Tell me something fucked up about your past," she says, nuzzling against me. "Something you've never told anyone else before."

"Okay," I say, clearing my throat. "My stepdad told me he'd divorce my mom if I didn't play football."

"Are you serious?"

"Yep."

"I don't understand. What would you playing football have to do with his marriage?" she asks.

"See, the thing about Mark is ..." I smirk. "He's a loser. He's also a user. He met my mother when she was a widowed single mom sitting on a fat stack of cash from my father's life insurance policy. He, too, was a single parent who had just lost his spouse. So he weaseled his way into her life by showing her how wonderful this new little family of theirs could be together and part of that was playing the role of super dad to me. My mom was beyond impressed by how attentive he was with me, and she loved the idea of being able to give me a father figure. But what started out as the two of us playing catch in the backyard a few nights a week morphed into flag football and local leagues and competitive leagues and by the time I got to junior high, he had me working with former NFL players, dropping thousands of dollars on coaches and clinics—anything he could do to push me to be the best ... because that was *his* dream. He'd just accepted a full-ride to San Diego State playing football when he tore his ACL. Never made a full recovery. Lost his scholarship, lost his dream of a career playing pro football."

"So you were his surrogate."

"Exactly. And when I told him I was tired of the game, tired of eating, sleeping, and breathing football, he lost his fucking mind," I say. "He knew how much I loved my mom and he knew I'd never do anything to hurt her. She was crazy about him. Still is. The man deserves an Oscar because he can play that husband-of-the-year role better than anyone. You know, once I walked in on him fucking his secretary in his office. Mom sent me to drop off some dinner since he claimed he was working late."

Irie pulls a breath between her teeth.

"I never told her," I say. "And I don't know that I will. But only because it doesn't take much to set her over the edge. She's fragile like that. It's why she's always self-medicating."

"Has she always been like that?"

"I don't think so. From what I've been told, losing my dad was pretty traumatic for her." I gaze up at the starry sky that blankets us. "She was never the same after she lost him. He was the love of her life."

Silence settles between us as we lose ourselves in our own thoughts for a while. The conversation tonight is heavy, but opening up to her floods me with a lightness I've never known before.

"Did you mean it when you said you hated football?"

she asks. "The other week ... at your house ..."

"I don't know. I used to love it. And a part of me still does. But when something is forced on you for years and years and you don't have a say in the matter, sometimes that love turns into resentment."

"Don't let him steal that from you," she says, hoisting herself up on her elbow to look me in the eyes. "You're insanely gifted. Don't throw that away because of him. If you loved football once, you can love it again."

"Yeah, but it's stolen everything from me," I say, my mind going to the contract I still have yet to sign. "And now it's going to steal you."

Irie buries her head against my shoulder. There isn't anything she can say that hasn't already been said, any thought she could share that hasn't already passed through both of our minds.

"Sometimes I wish I didn't get that Richmond offer," I confess. "I kept holding out and holding out last fall after the first several offers, thinking they'd eventually stop coming as the rosters filled. But then Richmond dropped this in my lap. Literally an offer too good to pass up. But all I can think about is how easy it would be to walk away."

"You can't do that."

"Now you sound like Mark ..."

"That's not what I mean," she says. "You've been giving this once-in-a-lifetime opportunity, Talon. You have these gifts, these talents. Use them for good. The world is exceeding capacity on assholes and you have a chance to be one less asshole in the world. Imagine all the wonderful things you could do with that money, with your fame and your image. You could be someone's *hero*. Lord knows the world doesn't have enough of those. I mean ... kids will be wearing your jersey, hanging posters of you on their walls and saying they want to be like you someday. And they should be. Because you're so much more amazing than anyone realizes—and I'd hate to see the world miss out on that."

"You make it sound so nice," I say. "But there's still a missing piece to all of that."

"You don't have to love football now. You can learn to love it again."

"That's not what I'm talking about, Irie," I say. "You're the missing piece in that beautiful picture you just painted." I pull her over top of me, her long legs straddling my sides, and I sit up. "I want those things, Irie. I want to be that man. But I want you too." She tries to respond, but I silence her with a kiss, my fingers slipping through her caramel strands. My cock throbs, straining against the inside of my jeans. I've never felt this close to anyone in my life and yet it's not enough. I want more of her.

Deeper, harder, more

"I'm falling for you, Irie," I whisper. "And I want you to know ... I would *never* use you. I would never make you feel ashamed for enjoying something you have every right to enjoy ..."

She kisses me back, her body melting against mine.

"I love you." The words glide off my tongue, effortless and with an autonomy of their own, and nothing I've ever said has felt so right, but maybe that's because they've been there all along, from the moment I laid eyes on her.

I've never believed in love at first sight, soulmates, or any of that bullshit—but that was before Irie Davenport walked into my life.

She pulls away, cupping my face in her gentle hands and depositing her wistful gaze on mine. "I ... I love you too."

CHAPTER 31

Irie

WE LIE UNDER THE STARS, basking in silence and our shared confessions and new admissions. It doesn't feel right to say anything more, to taint the complicated beauty of tonight with small talk.

"We should head back," I say, gazing at a darkened sky. I don't feel like dealing with my aunt's wrath if I stay out too late. Despite the fact that I'm a grown woman, I'm staying at their house and fully expected to respect that curfew.

We stroll the three blocks back to my aunt and uncle's house hand in hand relatively unrushed, and we stop at the rental car at the end of the driveway. All the other cars that were here earlier appear to be long gone and the house is mostly dark save for a few inside lights.

"I should probably go check into my room," he says, his fingers twisted with mine as we face one another. "You're welcome to stay with me ..."

He made that same offer before, and as much as I'd love it, I can't. "I need to stay with Bette."

"All right," he says, sighing as he leans in and tastes my mouth one last time tonight. "Call me in the morning."

I amble up the driveway as he climbs into the driver's side of the Nissan, and I sneak inside, reeling.

Every part of me is lit, alive in a way I've never known.

I feel unstoppable, giddy, and I couldn't wipe this ridiculous smile off my face if I tried.

It's a foreign sensation—all of it, but it doesn't take long for me to realize …

… this must be what it feels like to be loved.

CHAPTER 32

Talon

WE FILE into a pew in the middle of the church Saturday afternoon, next to a woman with an oversized hat and a man in a mothball-scented tweed suit. Their expressions are somber, mournful almost. But I think that's just the way they look ...

The place is covered in pale pink flowers and silver ribbons and a woman in the front plays *How Great Thou Art* on an organ. Irie says this is what weddings are like in Iron Cross—a hybrid between a marriage ceremony and a service, but with an odd funeral vibe to round it out.

"You excited?" Irie asks with a teasing wink. "You seem like the kind of guy who just loves a good Midwestern wedding."

"Let's be real: I'm just here to catch the bouquet."

She laughs through her nose, but her smile fades the moment her attention skirts over my shoulders toward a clean-cut dark-haired man making his way down the aisle.

He takes a seat in the row behind us, a leggy brunette with glossy curls on his arm. The stench of his overpowering perfume is almost nauseating as it assaults the air around us. Irie's hand is still in mine, only there's a slight tremble to it.

It's him.

Trey McAvoy.

Has to be.

I don't think she's afraid of him—I think his sheer presence brings out all the deep shit she's been avoiding all these years.

I give her hand a tight squeeze before leaning in and whispering, "Fuck that guy."

Her posture gives a little, and she relaxes against me, resting her head against my shoulder.

"I love you," I whisper next.

"I love you too."

Saying those words to her last night in the football field was the scariest fucking thing I've ever done—but once they were out, I'd never felt so liberated.

So I'm *that* guy now.

Drunk-in-love, drunk on *her*.

After a few more minutes, the pews fill all the way to the back, and the groom makes his way up front next to the preacher.

As soon as the music begins to change, five sets of bridesmaids and groomsmen march down the aisle, all of them carbon copies of one another. Honestly with as prissy and conniving as Lauren is, I'm shocked she was able to scrounge up these many friends for her bridal party.

Irie keeps her attention on the front of the church, her gaze never veering, not once. But every time I steal a quick look around, I catch him staring, watching the two of us. I even shoot him a smile. Not a kind one of course, one that implies that I see him, I'm onto him. That she's mine. That he can gawk all he wants but she'll never want him, she'll never be his again.

His gaze is so heavy, so penetrating, so invasive, I'm going to need a chemical shower to get it all off me.

As soon as the bridal party is settled up front, the music changes once again, the wooden pews creaking as everyone rises to acknowledge the bride. In the back of the church, Lauren stands in the whitest of white princess-style gown. An elaborate veil covers her face, hiding everything but her bright pink lips that match the plethora of pink flowers she's had placed in every corner of the sanctuary.

A woman in front of us gasps when Lauren and her father pass, exclaiming to her husband that Lauren looks like a "modern-day Grace Kelly" ... whoever that is.

A few moments later, Michael gives his daughter away and takes a seat next to Elizabeth in the front row, dabbing at the corners of his watering eyes.

It makes me think of Irie—and the fact that she doesn't have a dad. Would she want Michael to give her away someday? Or maybe she doesn't want to marry at all. Seems like everyone I know is swearing off marriage, and for a while, I was right there alongside them.

But when you meet someone and you know you want to spend the rest of your life with them, it changes your whole perspective on locking it down.

I glance at Irie, whose stoic expression is virtually unreadable, and I'd give anything to know what she's thinking right now ... specifically, if she's thinking the same thing I'm thinking.

THEY HOLD THE RECEPTION—IF you can even call it that—in the church basement. There's no DJ. No bar. Just "refreshments," a wedding cake, and an overflowing folding table covered in gifts for the newlyweds.

"They don't believe in dancing," Irie says to me as we scan the large fellowship hall. "It's against their religion."

"I mean, I get not wanting to blast Bruno Mars songs in God's house and all of that, but I've never heard of dancing being against anyone's religion."

"It's too seductive," she says, her tone nonplussed. "Might encourage premarital relations."

"Anyone who thinks dancing is too seductive has never seen my Grandma Mary breaking it down to Motown Philly."

She laughs at my cheesy one-liner and bats me on the shoulder. "I'm going to go find Aunt Bette and get us a table before they all fill up. You want to grab us some cake and sparkling cider?"

"I'm on it."

Irie disappears into the crowded room and I head toward the refreshments table, where the line is already eight people deep.

I'm minding my own business, waiting my turn, when some guy behind me clears his throat like he's trying to get my attention. Curious, I glance back and find him.

The asshole of the hour—no, the asshole of the century.

"You're here with Irie, right?" he asks, hands clasped in front of him as he puffs out his chest. His tone is a desperate attempt to be cool and friendly but his rigid posture and defensive stance are a glaring contradiction.

He's intimidated by me.

Maybe even jealous.

Which makes no sense seeing how he threw Irie away like fucking trash after she gave him the night of his life.

The more I stare at this smug bastard's pinched-in face, the tighter my fists clench. If I don't get some goddamned wedding cake in my hands in the next fifteen seconds, it's not going to look good for him.

"I, uh … we used to date," he says, with a nervous chuckle, like I'm supposed to find that cute.

"Yeah," I say. "I know."

His thin lips crack into a proud smile. "She stills talks about me, doesn't she?"

I don't know if it's the arrogant funk permeating off his body or the fact that he thinks I'm dumb enough to believe he's simply making conversation here and not trying to infiltrate his nose in his ex-girlfriend's business, but a flash of heat sears through me and my palms begin to twitch.

"We had a pretty bad falling out in the end," he says, leaning in like it's some kind of secret between us. "Always wondered what happened to her. She left Iron Cross after graduation and never came back. Always wondered if it had to do with me."

I flatten my lips to keep from saying what I really want to say, and the cake line moves ahead.

"Honestly, I've known her for years and the first time she ever mentioned you was last night," I say.

He chuffs, rolling his eyes. "Yeah, right."

"Why would I lie to you about that? I don't even know you. And honestly, I don't know why you're talking to me right now. If I were you, I'd be staying as far away as I could."

His self-satisfied smirk vanishes. I can only assume he's spent the last four years fantasizing about how much she was missing him, relishing in the fact that he thought he had the upper hand in the break up. I bet not once did he imagine her showing up to Lauren's wedding completely smitten with someone new.

Leaning in, Trey sniffs. "You don't scare me."

I scratch at my temple before crossing my arms, sizing him up once more, examining a loose thread sticking out from the shoulder of his cheap suit jacket.

This dude is all for show.

He doesn't care about being a decent person as long as he looks the part. On the inside, he's just as fake and rotten as the nasty cologne he drowned himself in before he came here.

The line moves once more.

"Hey," Irie's voice calms the moment and I turn to my right to find her standing next to me. "I got us a table. Just seeing if you needed some help. Aunt Bette wants a piece of—"

Her eyes widen when she notices Trey.

"Hey, Irie," he says, his mouth sliding into a slick grin ... one I'd love nothing more than to smack off his self-righteous face. "Been a long time."

I don't know if Irie is verbally paralyzed in his presence or if she's simply trying to take the high road by not engaging with this jackass, but she turns her back to him, like he isn't even there, and for some reason I find it fucking hilarious.

I slip my hand into hers and the line moves once again.

And then I hear the word "slut" ... clear as day ... from Trey's mouth.

It happens so fast—my balled fist coming into contact with the midline of his perfectly straight nose.

One clean slice of a punch and the jackass falls to the floor.

A woman screams.

Two men rush to his aid.

Irie slips her hands around my bicep, tugging me away from the scene as her uncle sprints across the crowded room.

There's blood everywhere. Apparently the fucker bleeds easily. Someone yells for ice, another person yells for towels.

"We have to get out of here," Irie says as her uncle pushes and shoves his way through the gathering crowd of worked-up wedding guests.

"You two!" he points at us—like she's equally to blame for what just happened.

I lift a hand in protest as we back away. "We're leaving."

Irie takes me past the table where Aunt Bette is saving our spots and grabs her phone and little black clutch.

"What's going on?" Bette asks, squinting across the room toward the circle of people trying to help poor, defenseless Trey McAvoy.

"Talon punched Trey," Irie says. "We have to go."

Bette's face lights up and her hands clap, and before I know it, she's rising from the table to give me an actual standing ovation. "Bravo, Talon. Bravo. I knew I liked you."

"Bette, I'll call you later," Irie tells her before navigating us out of the fellowship hall, up the wooden stairs, and out the back door to the parking lot, where our Nissan chariot awaits.

My fist throbs, and my heart ricochets the way it does during the final seconds of the fourth quarter.

"I can't believe you did that," she says, breathless, her palm splayed across her forehead.

"I'm sorry. After what he said, I couldn't stand back and—"

"No, don't apologize," she says, waving her hand. "That's not what I meant. I mean ... I've been fantasizing about punching him in the face for years and you did it!"

Irie throws her arms around me, bouncing on her toes.

"Thank you," she whispers, her face buried against my neck. A moment later, she kisses me, soft and slow, her lips curling against mine. "Take me to your hotel. I don't think I can wait any longer ..."

CHAPTER 33

Irie

MY HEART BEATS in my ears as he unlocks the hotel room door. We step into a dark void, wrapped in a blanket of icy air that sends a thrill down my spine.

"You sure this is what you want?" he asks as the door floats shut behind us.

"Yes."

He reaches for a light switch and a small lamp next to the king-sized bed illuminates. The suite is luxurious and contemporary—not your average Peony Falls, Missouri hotel room, and he curls his finger around mine, leading me to the foot of the bed.

Once there, he sits on the edge and pulls me into his lap. The hem of my dress rides up, inviting him to slide his palms up my bare flesh.

Originally I never intended to take things this far with him. It was never supposed to get physical. But then he held me in his arms last night and absorbed my sordid past with zero judgement, and when it was over, he told me he loved me.

And punching Trey at my cousin's wedding? Well, that was the icing on the cake.

"I love you, Irie," his words are delivered on cinnamon breath while his hands slide beneath my dress until he finds my panties. His movements are slow, deliberate. I don't know why I expected the first time with him to be animalistic. Of course it wouldn't be—the man is going to savor me, savor this moment.

Talon shrugs out of his suit jacket and leans back on the bed. I climb over him as he slides my panties down to my ankles, tossing them aside. A moment later, his hands cup my ass and he pulls me against him, my bare sex rocking against the outline of his throbbing cock that grows harder by the second.

I slide my dress over my shoulders and his hands travel up my back until he reaches the clasp of my strapless bra. Within seconds it's gone, vanished into the dark void of the hotel room.

"You're so fucking sexy," he says, sitting up and taking a pert nipple between his lips as his hands continue to explore this newfound territory. He stops to kiss me, his tongue fondling mine, and a minute later he flips me to my back, crawling over my naked body. His mouth presses hot kisses against my collarbone, working his way between my breasts before traveling down my stomach, which caves against his touch. The faintest hint of his five o'clock shadow tickles my sensitive skin, and I reach down to run my fingers through his hair as I get comfortable.

A moment later, he's kissing my inner thigh, moving closer and closer to the ache between my legs. Closing my eyes, I sink into the mattress, my body overcome with tiny earthquakes as the heat of his breath centers on the one place I want it most.

When the flick of his tongue dances across my seam, I let out a sigh, gripping a handful of sheets. He teases a finger down my slit before taking another taste, and another. With his corded steel arms hooked around my thighs, he pulls me closer to the edge of the bed, lowering himself to his knees and making a meal out of me.

I'm flushed with arousal, high as a kite on anticipation as he devours me, taking his time and bringing me to the edge and back more times than I can count.

It's getting harder to fight the wave that wants to wash over me, each peak growing more intense than the one before. Finally I reach below, placing my hand over his, and I release a surrendered breath.

His heat leaves my thighs and he rises over me, his hand moving to his belt. I sit up to help him, my fingers tugging on his zipper, my hands grazing the swollen bulge in his suit pants. He lowers his mouth against mine, depositing a biting kiss that tastes like my arousal and his sweet tongue all at once.

My heart ricochets as I take his veined cock in my hands a moment later, pumping the length as he stares deep into my eyes. A second later, I bring myself to the floor, the hotel carpet rough against my knees, and I take him in my mouth.

Talon moans, his hands making fists in my hair, and I take him deeper, faster.

"I can't wait another fucking minute, Irie," he says.

I wipe the corner of my mouth, gazing up at him.

"I have to have you." He takes my hand, helping me back to the bed, climbing over me. "I have to have you right now."

He presses my thighs apart, settling between them and

running his finger along my slit before pressing it gently inside me. I squirm with his touch, my mind impatient but my body responsive, and I bite my lower lip.

"I don't have a condom, Irie," he says, exhaling.

"What?" I sit up on my elbows, squinting at him through the dim light.

"Believe it or not, I don't carry them with me."

"You don't use them or ..."

"I don't sleep around," he says. "I haven't been with anyone since my freshman year, since before I saw you."

The heat from my naked body teases the heat from his. We're so close—yet so far away.

"I've never slept with anyone without a condom," I tell him. "Have you?"

"Never."

I can't believe I'm about to suggest this but given the fact that I just finished my period three days ago, I think it's safe to say I'm not ovulating anytime soon.

"Do you ... do you want to just ... pull out?" I propose.

He worries the inner corner of his lip. "Are you sure? You sure you're okay with that?"

I nod, slow. "I am if you are."

His gaze holds on mine for what feels like forever, and then he settles between me, his hands running up my thighs as his throbbing cock presses against my sex. Bracing myself, I swallow the lump in my throat and wrap my legs around him. With a hand around the base of his dick, he guides himself into my wetness, slowly, inch by inch.

Talon exhales as he fills me to the hilt, the pain of the initial stretch morphing into sheer pleasure as my body accepts his. I dig my nails into his back as he settles into a rhythm, stopping to steal a kiss every so often. His cock is warm inside me, velvet soft, setting every last nerve ending on fire with want.

"God, you feel so good," he says, his voice breathy against my ear. "I could stay inside you all night ..."

My body shudders as I fight off another intoxicating wave I'm not ready to ride yet. Heat sears through my body in flashes and a fullness floods my center. It's a strange feeling. Distinct. Almost indescribable.

I never had this with Trey—or anyone else for that matter.

I'm guessing this is what it feels like to sleep with someone you love, someone who loves you.

"Don't stop," I whisper, running my fingers through his hair as my hips buck against him, thrust for thrust.

Biting my lip, I squeeze my eyes as he drives into me faster, harder, deeper.

I should be one hundred percent focused on this moment, but already I'm thinking of round two.

And there *will* be a round two.

Maybe even a three ...

We're supposed to fly out in the morning.

Looks like we'll be doing most of our sleeping on the plane.

CHAPTER 34

Talon

"I'M GOING to grab a quick shower," Irie says, wrapped in my bedsheets. It's the first Monday of spring break—which puts the biggest stupid smile on my face because it means one full week of having Irie all to myself, no classes, no quizzes, nothing but time on our hands. "Told Brynn I'd meet her for lunch today."

The thought of Irie doing her own thing for a couple of hours today makes me irrationally jealous of her best friend, but I push it away. It's not like she won't come back to me. I've just been spoiled the last few days with not having to share me.

As soon as our plane touched California ground yesterday, we couldn't grab our shit fast enough.

I took Irie and Bette home first so Irie could help her unpack and get settled, but it wasn't long before she was back at my door—and in my arms—ready for another round.

I tug the sheets off her as she scampers away, stealing a

greedy look at her perfect ass as she prances off to the bathroom with sex hair and an exhausted smirk. A second later the shower spray spits to life and I pull myself out of bed, heading to the kitchen to make a couple of coffees for us.

Both of my roommates are gone—they left sometime over the weekend for Cabo. It's the first time in years I opted not to join them, but I can say with one hundred percent certainty that I made the right call.

I pop the first pod into the coffeemaker and grab a mug. While the machine percolates, I peek into the fridge to see what we have to eat. It's slim pickings, most of it with questionable expiration dates. Looks like we might be eating out this morning ...

The first coffee finishes and I swing the fridge door shut, but the second I turn to walk away, there's a knock at the door.

I check the clock on the microwave before deciding to ignore it. It's probably some place trying to slide pizza menus under the door or some shit.

I switch out the pods and mugs and press the brew button for the next cup.

Only the asshole knocks again.

Louder.

Harder.

"Talon, I know you're home." And then he says my name. "Open up. It's Mark. We need to talk."

Jaw tight, I force a breath through flared nostrils. If I ignore him, he's not going to go away ... he's going to let himself in.

He has the master key to every apartment in this entire building because he owns the place.

Exhaling again, I head to the door. I'd rather let him in

myself than put Irie through some kind of family drama shit show staring Mark Masterson.

"Yeah?" I answer the door in nothing but a pair of navy sweats, one hand cocked on my hip.

"I called you all weekend," he says.

"I know. I was out of state."

Mark pushes his way into the apartment, pacing the small kitchen and glancing around like he's looking for something.

"Can I help you with something?" I ask, scratching at my right temple.

"You haven't signed the contract yet," he says.

"I know."

"It expires this week. The hell kind of stunt are you trying to pull here?" Spittle flies with each syllable and his tan skin turns a shade of cherry almost instantly.

"Tal, I had to use the last clean towel," Irie's voice floats from around the corner, and a second later, she appears in the hallway, a white towel wrapped around her taut body, hair dripping wet. "Oh my God. I'm so sorry."

She scampers off, disappearing into my room and leaving nothing but a wake of thick tension in the air.

"Is *that* what this is all about?" he asks, sneering.

"No," I lie.

Kind of.

My reasons are rooted much deeper than Irie, deeper than he could begin to realize, and I'm not in the mood to shoot the shit with my good ol' stepdad over any of it right now.

"I'm still figuring out a few things," I say.

"What's there to figure out, Talon?" Mark throws his hands in the air, the whites of his eyes visible all the way around. "Don't be a goddamned moron. Don't throw away everything we've worked for over a fucking *girl*. You know how much tits and ass you're going to be getting, kid? She's nothing. One of these days, you probably won't even remember her name."

My teeth grit. "Leave."

"Sign the contract, Talon," he says. "Or else."

"Or else what? You're going to leave my mom?" I scoff. "That might have worked on me when I was a kid, but that was before I knew how ugly and complicated a California divorce can be ... especially when it comes to splitting up assets, and especially when one of you has been habitually unfaithful to the other."

He wrinkles his stout nose. "The hell are you talking about?"

"I'm talking about Dierdre ... Cara ... Hollie ... Becca," I say. "Want me to keep going? Because I can."

Mark turns a deeper shade of crimson than before. His thin lips move but nothing comes out.

"That's what I thought," I say, walking back to the door and swinging it open. "Like I said, Mark, I'm figuring some shit out and you need to leave. *Now*."

He puffs his barrel chest and storms out the door, slamming it so hard behind him it rattles the apartment windows.

I give myself five deep breaths in an attempt to calm myself down, and then I make my way to the bedroom, where Irie is perched on the edge of my bed, fully dressed as she combs through her damp hair.

"What was that all about?" Irie asks.

"Nothing," I say. "Just Mark being Mark."

CHAPTER 35

Irie

I SWITCH a load of clothes from Aunt Bette's washer to her dryer Tuesday morning when my phone rings. A strange number flashes across the screen, but the area code is local. I'm tempted to answer it out of sheer curiosity ... and I almost don't ...

"Hello?" I catch it on the final ring.

"Irie?" a woman asks.

"This is she ..."

"Irie, hi, it's Camilla," she says with a chuckle in her voice. "Camilla Masterson. Talon's mom ..."

"Oh, yes! Of course," I say. "Hi, how are you?"

I shut the dryer door and press the start button before leaning against the counter, phone pressed hard to my ear. I have no idea why Talon's mom would be calling me out of the blue like this or what she could possibly want. His birthday is in July, so it isn't that. Easter's a solid month away, so I doubt she's inviting me to some family dinner.

"I'm doing well, sweetheart," she says. "I was just calling because I'm going to be in the area this week and I thought maybe the two of us could meet for brunch? Just a ladies' thing?"

I'm speechless at first, then flattered. The fact that Talon's mom wants to spend time with me solo makes me wonder if he's told her how he feels about me. Maybe she wants to get to know me better?

"That's really kind of you, Camilla," I say. "I'm pretty free all week, so shoot me a text when you're heading my way and we'll make it happen."

"Wonderful!" she says. "If not tomorrow, it'll be the day after."

"Sounds great." I end the call, grab a basket of whites, and head to the kitchen to start folding.

"Well, hey there, stranger," Aunt Bette says as she sorts the mail next to the microwave.

"Are you teasing me or guilt tripping me?" I ask. "Because I probably deserve both ..."

I didn't intend to become so joined at the hip with Talon.

I also didn't intend to fall in love with him.

We're in that stupid-in-love phase where you're only thinking about each other, woefully addicted and barely alive until you get your next fix.

"Neither," Bette says with a wink. "I'm happy for you, Irie. I am. And you're still making time for all my chores and errands, so I've got nothing to complain about. It's a little quieter around here, that's all. Don't let me hold you back. Can't say I'd be doing it any different if I were in your shoes. Just glad to see you're having fun for once."

I fold a towel and place it aside. "You know ... his mom just called me."

"Oh, yeah?"

"She wants to do brunch ... just the two of us."

"She's scoping you out," Bette says.

"You think?"

She nods, brows lifted. "She must know her son is crazy about you, so she wants to get to know you a little better. It's both a courtesy thing and a precaution."

"Too bad she's wasting her time," I say, mumbling under my breath as I fold another fluffy towel. "Two more months and I'm going to Malibu and he's going to Richmond."

Bette sighs. "I'm sure this isn't easy for you, but I just want you to know you're doing the right thing. You might be head over heels for this guy right now, but the worst thing you can do is rearrange your entire future over someone you just met—and I say that as someone with far too much experience in that arena. One minute you're turning down your third-grade teaching job to run off with a guy who looks an awful lot like a young Burt Reynolds and the next minute you're managing a cockroach-infested strip joint."

I know she's right.

But it doesn't stop me from wishing she was wrong.

CHAPTER 36

Talon

"COME WITH ME," I say Wednesday night as we lie naked in my bed in a quiet apartment that feels worlds away from reality.

"What? Where are you going?" she asks, sitting up a bit.

"Come with me to Richmond, I mean."

She lies back down, settling against my shoulder. "Talon ..."

"I'm serious, Irie. I can't walk away from that contract ... but I can't walk away from you either. I know I'm being selfish, but I'm putting it out there. Come out east with me. We can start a life out there. We won't have to say goodbye after graduation. We'll pack our things in a U-Haul and—"

"Shh." Irie places her finger over my mouth. "Let's just enjoy the time we have, okay?"

"You love me, right?"

"Of course."

"But you have no reservations about pulling the plug on this and going our separate ways in two months ..."

"Look, *this* wasn't supposed to happen." She rolls to her side, propping herself on her elbow as she studies me. "You talked me into a date and then you talked me into another date and then you told me you loved me and all of this is happening so fast ... and don't get me wrong, I'm loving every minute of it, but now you're asking me to walk away from my dream so you can live yours? Do you really think that's fair?"

"I know it isn't fair," I say. "But when you look at the logistics of it, you can find a design job anywhere in the country. I'm not going to find another thirty-five-million-dollar football contract so easily ..."

"So your dream is more important than mine."

"*No.*" I rub my eyes, gathering my thoughts. "This is all coming out wrong."

"Yes it is."

"I'm just trying to be rational about this. Logical. Whatever."

"Talon ..." Irie traces her fingertips along my bare chest, sighing. "We can't be logical with an emotion that knows no logic."

She's right.

"I'm sorry. I had to ask." I take her hand in mine, lifting it to my lips and kissing her delicate fingers. "Can you blame a man for wanting it all?"

"It's an impossible decision. Either way, one of us loses," she says. "And we both have too much at stake to gamble with something that isn't ..."

Her voice trails into nothing.

"Isn't a sure thing?" I ask.

She doesn't confirm.

She doesn't deny either.

"Nothing in this life will ever be a sure thing," I say. Silence consumes us, both of us lost in our own thoughts for a moment. "What do you want out of this life?"

Without hesitation, without giving it an extra thought, she answers, "A home of my own. A nice family. Stability. Meaning. The priceless things most people take for granted."

And there's my old friend, irony, showing his face once again.

I lean down, kissing her forehead. "Same, Irie ... exact same."

CHAPTER 37

Irie

I SLEEP IN THURSDAY MORNING, buried under Talon's covers as he rushes out the door to catch an eight o'clock workout at the student fitness center. While I admire his dedication and discipline, we've been staying up until the wee hours of the morning every night all week and I could use an extra hour of shuteye.

Only the second he's gone, my phone buzzes on his nightstand.

I reach across the bed, swiping it with an exhausted groan, and I flip the screen to find a text from his mother.

CAMILLA: Good morning, Irie! Brunch at 10 today? The Gilded Ivy?

I tap out a quick "sounds good ... see you then!" before realizing I completely spaced off telling Talon his mom had reached out to me earlier this week. It's not a huge deal though. I'll just have to tell him all about it afterwards.

Flinging the covers off, I grab my things and head out,

locking up behind me with the spare key Talon gave me. Within minutes, I'm making my way back home to shower and get ready, all the while contemplating the perfect outfit.

Camilla is stylish and polished, and a place called The Gilded Ivy requires more than a pair of faded jeans and a cute top from the back of my closet. I realize it's ironic ... wanting her to like me when I'm only going to be her son's girlfriend for the next two months, but it is what it is.

THE SECOND I step foot inside The Gilded Ivy, it reminds me of the kind of chic eatery one might find on Rodeo Drive in Beverly Hills. Everything is either gold or marble, but nothing about it is ostentatious. It's a tasteful kind of glamorous, and I give myself a mental pat on the back as I make my way to the hostess stand.

"I'm meeting Camilla Masterson," I tell the woman with the bun slicked so tight it gives my scalp sympathy pains.

Her magenta lips curl into a reserved smile. "Right this way, Ms. Davenport."

I follow her to a private room in the back, the kind people generally reserve for larger parties.

Camilla rises the instant she sees me, a pink boucle Chanel suit covering her trim body. "Irie, hi. So glad you could make it."

I take the seat across from her as a server appears from out of nowhere to fill my water glass and hand me a gold-leafed menu.

"Don't you look lovely," she says, eyeing my outfit. I opted for wide-leg black-waisted pants and a fitted white blouse, finishing off the look with simple gold hoops on my ears and a red statement lip—a look not unlike the one Kira Kepner was rocking the first time I met her.

"Thank you," I say. "I love your suit. Such a classic."

She runs her fingers along a fringed boucle sleeve. "Thank you. I couldn't decide between pink or ivory today ... anyway ..."

Camilla takes a sip from a champagne glass filled with orange juice and I think about what Talon said about his mom always self-medicating. She places it aside, her fingers tapping on the table. Despite the fact that she invited me to this brunch, I'm picking up on a little nervousness from her end.

"Are you enjoying your spring break?" she asks.

I smile. "Very much so. Talon and I caught that new Tarantino film the other day, and just yesterday, we volunteered at an animal shelter."

Her brows lift. "Talon ... my Talon ... volunteered?"

I pretend not to act surprised that she's surprised ...

From what it sounds like, growing up, he didn't have time to do anything but football. If he'd have been afforded a little more free time, I imagine he would've done amazing things with it.

"What about you? What have you been up to these days?" I hate small talk, but it's a necessary evil when you're trying to establish a rapport with someone.

She offers a polite smile, hesitating for a moment. "A little of everything I suppose ..."

And then I realize—she didn't come here to vet me. She didn't come here to get to know me. She came here with a mission.

"Irie, I'm going to cut to the chase here," she says. "The reason I invited you out to brunch is because Talon hasn't signed his contract yet."

"What?"

I had no idea ...

Just the other night he asked me to go with him to Richmond. I assumed he'd already signed the contract ...

"The deadline is tomorrow," she says. "If he doesn't sign it, they can take the offer off the table completely or they can give him a less ... savory ... offer."

"I had no idea. He hasn't told me any of this." There's a sharp stab in my middle, though I think the pain is all in my imagination, the emotional sting of betrayal.

Why wouldn't he have told me this? It's not the kind of thing that someone casually leaves out of conversation with their significant other, especially when we've talked about the future on several different occasions.

He always made it sound like he was going—so what's with the contract?

"I need you to end this with him," she says, sitting taller, her gaze cold and penetrating. Gone are her nerves and in their place is an agenda. "Immediately."

"Camilla ..."

"Irie, he's come too far to throw this all away, and I know you know that. You seem to be a very reasonable young woman with a good head on your shoulders, so I'm sure you understand the gravity of this situation," she says, taking another sip of her mimosa. "If you love my son, and I believe that you do, you'll end this. You'll let him go so he can sign the contract and do what's best for his future." She examines me before continuing. "And if he loves you, he'll wait for you, for the right time. If what you have is real, you'll be together again. Someday."

"I understand what you're saying, but I think he and I should talk about—"

"No," her voice cuts over mine and her shoulders

straighten. "This is the only way. I know my son. I know how relentless he can be with something he wants and I know how wild he is about you. You're going to have to call it off. It's going to have to be your decision, not something you decide together. If you love him, if you care about his future, you're going to have to break his heart."

My stomach twists until it burns. The thought of doing this to Talon tears me up inside.

I can't go behind his back and make this decision for him.

But I also know he shouldn't throw his entire future away for *me*.

There's a part of him that loves the game, even if he's temporarily misplaced that love.

I can't take that away from him.

I love him too much.

"You seem to be thinking about this," Camilla says, her full lips pressed into a hard line. "I was afraid of that." She clears her throat. "The first time we met, you mentioned you'd been offered a job with Kira Kepner, opening her new Malibu location."

"Yes ..."

"Kira actually started out as an intern of mine back in the day," she says, brushing a silky strand of hair off her cheekbone. "We're quite close. In fact, I'm quite close with a lot of people in this industry—particularly in the Southern California region. And Mark does quite a bit of business with a lot of them. It's quite an incestuous little industry. Anyway, a couple of phone calls, Irie, and your shiny new degree would be reduced to ash." Camilla clucks her tongue. "It'd be a shame seeing all those years, all that hard work, go to waste."

My eyes sting, but I refuse to cry in front of this woman.

Talon once described her as "fragile." When I met her, I thought she was quite effervescent, though maybe that was the sangria talking. Now I realize she's nothing more than a bully.

"I'm sorry, Camilla. I need to leave," I say, standing.

But she reaches across the table, covering my hand with hers. "I need this to happen by tomorrow or I'll be making a phone call to Kira, personally."

CHAPTER 38

Talon

"IRIE." I can't answer the door fast enough Thursday night. "I've been calling you all day. I thought something happened."

She isn't wearing her dimpled smile and she doesn't run into my arms, wrap her long legs around me, and greet me with a kiss.

Her hands grip the strap of her handbag and she swallows, keeping her gaze low.

"What happened? Are you okay?" I make a move for her arm to guide her inside since she's standing in the hall, still as a statue, but she jerks out of my reach.

"I'm sorry, Talon," she finally says. "I don't think we should date anymore."

None of this makes sense.

She was here this morning and last night and all day yesterday ... the night before that and the night before that.

"Is this because of what I asked you the other day?" I ask. "About moving to Richmond? Because if it is—"

"—no," she says. "We're just ... we're moving too fast and we know exactly where this is headed, so I think it's time we—"

"—no." It's my turn to interrupt this time. "I don't want that. Irie, you don't want that. I know you don't. What changed? What happened today?"

She checks her watch. "I have to go."

"Come in. Let's talk about this."

"There's nothing to talk about. I've made my decision." Her gaze avoids mine.

For the first time in a long time, I'm at a complete loss.

I can't force her to come inside. I can't force her to talk this out with me right now.

"I don't know what happened or what brought this on, Irie, but I know we've been spending a lot of time together. I know I came on strong in the beginning," I say. "If you want space, take it. If you want time to yourself for a bit, that's fine too. I'll still be here. I'm not going anywhere. No matter what happens, no matter what you decide, I'll still love you."

She tries to say something and stops, and I swear her lips tremble for a second.

"Goodbye, Talon," she says before turning to leave.

Space. She needs space.

And maybe some time.

But this isn't the end.

I won't allow it.

I refuse to make it this far, only to fumble the ball.

CHAPTER 39

Irie

I PULL Aunt Bette's Crown Vic to a stop at a light a couple blocks from Talon's place, my sight clouded with thick, salty tears.

I ended it.

But not because of Camilla.

I didn't do it for her and I didn't do it because she backed me into a corner.

I did it for him and only him.

I had no idea he hadn't signed the contract, but when Camilla dropped that on me, I knew exactly why: he's holding out for me.

As wonderful and magical and lovely as everything is when I'm with him, it's all so new, so uncertain. I can't be the reason he walks away from a once-in-a-lifetime opportunity.

Camilla said that if our love was real, we'd be together again someday. While that all sounds good and well, I know the instant he sets foot on Virginia soil and is handed that jersey, he's going to have his pick of the litter. Women will be lined up everywhere and he'll be coming fresh off a heartbreak, looking to screw his way into forgetting me.

I wipe a tear from my cheek, knowing that probably isn't true.

Talon isn't like that.

Once upon a time I thought he was ... but that was before I actually got to know him.

Under his arrogant façade and unapproachable persona is a good man, and one of these days another woman is going to recognize that in him and she's going to hold onto him for dear life, marry him and have all of his babies, and I'm just going to be a watercolor memory.

I swipe at another tear and another.

They refuse to stop.

And suddenly I'm pulling into Bette's driveway.

It's like I blinked and I was home, with no recollection of the drive here.

I kill the engine and check my phone—three missed calls, two voicemails and a text ... all from him.

I can't bring myself to listen to them so I delete them all, and then I silence my phone.

If I let myself hear him out, I know exactly what will happen. I'll change my mind and I'll ruin his future. Maybe not now, maybe not in the short term, but in the long run. I don't want to be the girl he threw it all away for.

I love him too much.

CHAPTER 40

Talon

"TALON," Ira damn near screams my name on the other side of the phone Friday morning. "The deadline is today. TO. DAY. Why the hell have you not signed anything yet?"

I exhale into the phone.

I didn't want to answer, but he'd already called me thirteen times this morning alone and he wasn't going to stop until he got through.

Irie left me last night.

All I've been doing since she walked away was replay every conversation, every word that ever came out of my mouth trying to figure out where I went wrong.

She won't answer her phone.

Won't reply to my texts.

I stayed up all night, tossing and turning in sheets that still smelled like her.

"You know they can drop the offer altogether," Ira

continues. "They could also chop it in half—and you'd still have to take it because even half of what they want to give you is twice as much as what anyone else wanted to give you. I'm sorry, kid. I love you, but you're a goddamned fool if you don't sign this thing."

He doesn't love me.

He only loves his fifteen percent—the six million he stands to gain the second my pen touches that signature line.

"Something like this will never happen for you again in your lifetime," he says. "You're not going to take a few years off, turn twenty-seven, and then magically find yourself with another multimillion-dollar offer from the pros. This is it, Tal. It's now or it's never. We're down to zero hour and you need to make a decision."

"I'm aware of all of that, Ira," I say, pinching the bridge of my nose as I pace my quiet apartment.

"Tell me ... why the sudden change of heart?" he asks. "Is it the girl? Is that what this is all about?"

I stop pacing. "I never told you about her."

He blows a puff of breath into his receiver. "Ah, come on. It's always about a girl when it comes to this shit."

"You've been talking to Mark, I see."

"Talon ..."

"As my agent, any communication needs to be directed toward me and only me. Not my fucking stepfather."

"I'm sorry, kid. You're right. It's just he called me the other day because he was concerned since you hadn't signed yet."

"Then you should have directed him to me."

"I tried. You know how he is."

"I know exactly how he is," I say. "I also know how you are. You're no pushover."

"Look, I get that you're upset and you have every right to be, and I'm sorry for that. At the end of the day, we're all just trying to look out for you, trying to make sure you don't throw away your future."

Oh my God.

I don't know why I hadn't thought of it before but it makes perfect sense now ... Irie dumping me on the eve of my contract deadline has Mark written all over it.

"I have to go," I tell Ira when he's mid-spiel, still trying to cover his ass.

"Talon. You have to sign by three o'clock today or it's all over. If you—"

I end the call, grab my car keys, and head across town to Bette's. I thought time and space were all she needed, but now that I know her hand was forced into dumping me, it changes everything.

She didn't want to leave me.

She felt like she had no choice.

I fly into Bette's driveway, shift into park, and hurry toward the front door, knocking like a crazy person until the door swings open.

Only it isn't Irie.

"Bette," I say. "I need to talk to Irie—and before you tell me she isn't here—"

"She isn't here," Bette says, point blank. "Feel free to take a look around if you don't believe me."

"Where is she?"

"Said she was going to go work on some project for one of her classes. Last I saw her, she had her bag and she was walking to the bus stop. I imagine she's on campus. Check the design lab maybe? I know she hangs out there quite a bit. Or she did before she met you ..."

Bette isn't in an overly friendly mood—which makes me

wonder what she knows—but the fact that she didn't shut the door in my face is a good sign.

"Thanks, Bette," I say as I trek back to my car.

Backing out, I head to campus to find my girl.

CHAPTER 41

Irie

I WANDER around campus in a daze most of Friday morning. We're on the cusp of spring and everything's coming alive, only I don't see it.

It's all gray to me.

The color, the life, it's been sucked out of my world.

Every time I close my eyes, I see his face ... specifically the look on his face when I told him it was over. The light went out in his eyes and his smile faded, and the instant they were gone I wanted more than anything to be able to put them back, to see the face of the man who stole my heart when I least expected it.

I take a seat on a bench outside the Mercer Campanile, which lets out ten melancholy chimes.

I called Brynn earlier to see if she was around, but she had to cover a shift this morning at the print shop in campus town. I didn't tell her about Talon. I will later, but it didn't seem right to drop it so casually via text.

I tried to kill some time in the design lab earlier, working ahead on an upcoming project due at the end of the month, but I couldn't focus and every configuration I designed paled in comparison to my normal work.

Leaning back, I stare at the picturesque PVU campus, which for two short months of my life was heaven on earth.

I think about Talon's mother, her threats and her manipulations.

If Talon and I would've been given a chance to discuss this on our own, I imagine we would've reached the same decision—we would have agreed to go our separate ways ... for now. But the fact that that decision was made for us the way that it was is a fact I can't get over.

I keep replaying my conversation with Camilla in my mind, over and over, each time growing angrier, each time wanting to tell Talon the truth.

But I can't do that.

He needs to sign, he needs to embrace his future without me because he's going to do amazing things with it.

I just wish we could've had more time together.

CHAPTER 42

Talon

SHE ISN'T in the design lab.

Or the library.

She isn't in Meyers Commons or the armory.

I've walked the campus for hours ...

She isn't here.

"Just go ask him," I hear a woman whispering from behind me.

"I don't want to bother him," a guy whispers back.

"I'm sure he won't mind ..." she argues. "Just ask him to take a quick selfie with you ..."

I glance behind and find a baby-faced high school kid and his mom staring my way. The guest badges hanging from their neck mean they're touring the campus. The kid freezes when we lock eyes. Either he's starstruck or shy as hell.

I've never been a fan of selfies and the last thing I want to do is be bothered about a picture from some kid who looks like he's probably going to end up with MIT instead of PVU, but then I think about Irie and that silly little speech she gave me about being someone's hero someday.

"You want a pic?" I ask. "Give me your phone."

"What?" The kid's eyes widen and he glances around him, as if I'm talking to someone else.

"Get up there, Ronnie, take a pic with Talon Gold!" His mom shoos him toward me.

"Come on, Mom. You need to get in here too," I say, forcing a smile that takes all the energy I have.

She does a happy squeal before joining her son and they each hand me their phones.

I snap two pics and send them on their way.

I never would have done that shit before Irie.

She's changed me for the better, in ways I never could have anticipated.

Just wish she were here to see it ...

Nevertheless, I keep searching, and I won't stop until I find her.

CHAPTER 43

Irie

I BOOKMARK five Malibu rentals and fill out a handful of inquiry forms online. One of these weekends I'm going to have to drive up there and tour them in person, but for now I settle for photos.

I thought apartment hunting was going to be a good way to focus on my future, I thought making my plans all the more real would help me accept my fate.

But it only made me miss him more because every time I found something I thought he'd like—a built-in ice maker, a trendy bar down the street—I realized I wouldn't be able to tell him about it and that he'd never be able to see these places; not in screenshots, not in real life.

It's funny how life surprises you sometimes. Never in a million years did I think I'd have agreed to a date with Talon. Never in a billion years did I think I'd fall in love with him.

He wasn't who I thought he was.

He was so much more ...

Pushing my thoughts aside, I keep searching for the perfect place to call home.

The rental market in Malibu is slim pickings and rent is astronomical. Most of the places that claim they have ocean views only boast the kind of ocean views you find when standing on your tiptoes, leaning over your tiny balcony railing.

But I'd take that over Iron Cross, Missouri a million times over.

Kira said I could borrow some furniture from her stock until I'm able to get some things of my own. Her only caveat was that I professionally style everything—which is a given—so she can have her photographer snap pictures for her social media.

The campanile chimes twelve times.

I should probably catch the bus back to Aunt Bette's.

My stomach swirls, anxious at the thought of asking her if Talon stopped by today. Part of me hopes he did, the other part hopes he didn't.

With my bag in tow, I trek to the nearest bus stop and wait for the blue line bus.

If I'm going to get through these next two months, I need to toughen up and stop feeling sorry for myself. It's not the first time I've been floating on a breeze only to have life knock me down ... and it won't be the last.

Life has always, *always* been consistent like that.

I should be used to it by now.

CHAPTER 44

Talon

I RETURN HOME EXPECTING to walk into a quiet, empty apartment, only to find my living room couch occupied by three of the last people I want to see right now.

"Get out," I say to Mark, Ira, and my mother.

They exchange looks, none of them trying to move. On the coffee table in front of them is a stack of white papers with Richmond's logo along the masthead.

"What is this, a fucking contract intervention?" I ask.

"Sweetheart, we're only trying to help." Mom is the first to break their silence. She stands, gingerly making her way across the room to where I stand, but when she gets here, she keeps a careful distance, like she's dealing with some kind of unstable basket case.

And maybe they are.

They took the one thing I loved, the first thing I ever truly loved, and ripped her out of my life without warning.

"All of your dreams are about to come true, Talon," Mom says. "All you have to do is sign."

I think about what Irie said last weekend, that I loved the game once, I can love it again. Deep down I know she's right. I could sign the contract, I could love the game again. But standing here, in front of three people who couldn't give a shit less about what I love and what I want, makes the idea of giving in a bitter pill to swallow.

"Don't you mean all of *Mark's* dreams?" I shoot him a look. Funny how quiet he's being. I imagine the little bombshell I dropped on him earlier this week has got him feeling tongue-tied today. "Fuck football. And fuck you, Mark."

"*Talon.*" Mom gasps, her hand splaying over her chest. "I don't understand what's going on. It's like ever since you met that girl, you've become a different person."

"Don't put this on her." My words slice through the small apartment. "Leave her out of this."

"We get that you loved her," she says.

"Love," I correct her. "I *love* her."

"Honey, I know you're hurting right now and break ups are never easy, but—"

I knew it.

I fucking *knew* it.

"What did you say to her?" I ask. "Huh? What'd you say to get her to leave me?"

She turns back to Mark, who gives a subtle shake of his head. I'm sure whatever she said, whatever she did, Mark was the puppet master behind it all.

"*What. Did. You. Do?*" I ask again, teeth gritted.

"Talon ..." Mom looks like she's two seconds from turning on the waterworks, but I don't have time for this shit.

So I leave.

I go.

I get in my car and I drive to Bette's—again.

And if Irie's still not home, I'll sit and wait.

Fifteen minutes later, I'm trotting up Bette's walkway and knocking on the door. The sound of footsteps on the other side is a relief, even if they don't belong to Irie.

"Hello again," Bette says when she answers.

"Irie isn't back by chance, is she?" I ask, realizing how breathless and worked up I am.

"Oh. Um ..." Bette presses her lips into a thin line. "I don't know that this is such a good time for a visit, Talon. Maybe try again another—"

"Aunt Bette, it's fine," Irie interrupts, stepping out from behind her great aunt. "I've got this. It's okay."

"You sure?" she asks. I look past Bette to find her friend, Brynn, in the mix as well. It kills me to think about what she's been going through today, all of it at the hands of Mom and Mark.

Irie nods as she makes her way out to the front stoop and Bette closes the door behind her.

"I don't know what they said to you, Irie," I begin. "But whatever it is, you don't have to listen to them. This ... *us* ... it's not their decision."

Her arms are folded and her gaze is steady on her bare feet.

"You know the other night when I asked what you wanted in life? Everything you listed off ... those are the things I want too," I say. "And I want them with you."

Her glassy eyes lift onto mine, but she doesn't say a word.

"You know why this is so complicated?" I ask. "Because it's real."

She's still quiet, contemplative.

"I want a future with you. And I don't know how to make that happen given our current circumstances, but it's something we have to figure out together," I say.

"Your mom threatened my career," she finally speaks. "She told me if I didn't leave you, she'd have me blacklisted. She even threatened to call Kira Kepner."

"Seriously?" Of all the things my mom is capable of, playing hardball like that, being ruthless, has never been her forte. "That has Mark written all over it."

"Why didn't you tell me you hadn't signed the contract yet?"

"I don't know ... because I hadn't made a decision yet."

"Were you planning to sign it at all?" she asks.

I shrug. "I don't know, Irie. I don't know."

"They said the deadline is today. Is that true?"

"Yes."

"You need to sign it." She lifts her chin, looking me square in the eyes. "Regardless of what your mother said, I love you too much to let you to throw your future away just to be with me."

"Come to Richmond. Start a life with me there."

"My job is in Malibu."

"I'll take care of you," I say.

She puffs a breath between her full lips. "I don't want to be taken care of. And this is my dream, my passion. I didn't go to college for four years just so I could do nothing."

"Then get a job in Richmond. Hell, I'll front you the money to start your own design firm."

"It's not the same."

Reaching for her, I untangle her folded arms and pull her nearer. "I don't understand. I'm offering you the world, I'm giving us options, and you're refusing to so much as consider any of it."

She bites at her trembling lip, glancing away.

"I have to sign that contract, Irie," I say, exhaling. "At the end of the day, I know it's a once-in-a-lifetime opportunity. I know I've worked for this my entire life. And you're right, somewhere, deep down, I fucking love the game. I was born to play, even if I've been feeling burnt out the last several years. But I also know that you're a once-in-a-lifetime opportunity. There's never going to be another you in my life, another us. So I'm asking you, one last time, to come with me. Let's build the best life together, you and me against the world. I'll give you that home you've always wanted, that stability and meaning you were talking about the other night."

She swipes at a tear that falls down her rosy soft cheek.

"I love you more than I've ever loved anything in the world," I say.

"And yet you barely know me."

"I know enough," I say. "And imagine how much more I'm going to love you when I get to know the rest of you." I manage to get the tiniest smile from her lips. "Please, Irie. I don't want to take Malibu away from you, but I can't walk away from this contract. And it's not because I want to be some rich, famous athlete. I keep thinking about what you said that night in Iron Cross ... about me being someone's hero someday. And I keep thinking about all the good I could do with that. Things that would make you proud. But I want to do those things with you by my side. You make me a better person. You bring out the best in me. I can't be that guy if I don't have you."

"Sure you can."

"My entire life, I was told to be a good ball player. You're the only person who's ever pushed me to be a good human being."

Irie pulls in a long, slow breath, staring deep into my eyes. "And what if it doesn't work out? What if I give up Malibu, move to Richmond, and by the end of the year we're sick of each other and you're sitting on the top of the world and I'm jobless and homeless and—"

"—Irie, Irie," I take her hands in mine. "Stop thinking about everything that could go wrong and start thinking about all the ways it's going to go right for us."

"You paint the most beautiful pictures with your words, Talon," she says. "And while I want all that, while it all sounds amazing ... you have to understand what a risk that would be for me. If this doesn't work, I have nothing. I have no one. You have a family, you come from money, you have a safety net that I don't have."

"Everything is a risk. You moving to Malibu is a risk. There's no guarantee that's going to work out either."

"You can't compare a job offer to a relationship ..."

"I didn't wait almost four years to finally have you, just to let you go. If I didn't care about you, I would've screwed you and walked away. I wouldn't be asking you to move to Virginia with me, to start a life together."

"Talon ..."

"You're terrified and I know that. But you need to trust me. Do you trust me, Irie?"

She considers my question, gazing up at me with uncertain eyes before finally offering a simple, "Yes."

Without saying another word, I lift my hand to her face, angle her mouth toward mine, and crush her lips with an owning kiss.

"I love you so damn much," I tell her. "I promise you, Irie, you're not going to regret this."

With that, I trot back to my car.

"Wait ... where are you going?" she asks, taking a few steps off the front stoop.

"I have a couple things I need to take care of," I call after her. "I'll get a hold of you tonight."

With that, I'm gone.

A man on a mission, I head back to my apartment, calling Ira on the way.

CHAPTER 45

Irie

"IRIE, WHAT BRINGS YOU IN TODAY?" Kira asks from her side of her desk Friday afternoon. "Everything okay?"

I take a seat across from her, crossing my legs and clearing my throat. "I'm afraid I'm going to have to turn down that job offer."

Kira's mouth is agape and her hands are splayed on her white-washed oak desktop. "What? What happened? Did you get a better offer somewhere else?"

"No, no," I say. "Your offer was ... extremely generous ... but—"

"—then what happened?" she asks, wild-eyed.

"I ... I know how this is going to sound," I say, half-chuckling. "And believe me, this isn't a decision I came to lightly ... but I met someone recently ... and he's asked me to move to Virginia with him after graduation."

"Oh, honey." Kira rests her chin on her hand, looking

like a big sister about to give her kid sister a talking to. "Are you sure this is what you want? You want to throw away your career over some boyfriend?"

"I'll be honest," I say. "I'm terrified."

She laughs.

"But I think this is something I need to do," I say.

Kira sighs. "I mean ... I get it. I guess. I've been there. I've been young and in love. I know what it's like when your heart speaks louder than your head. It just ... it blows for me, losing such talent. I was really looking forward to adding you to my team. I had big plans for you in Malibu."

My chest is heavy with that loss. "I know. I'm so sorry. I was excited about it too."

"Listen," she says, tucking her glossy onyx hair behind both ears before leaning closer. "If it doesn't work out with this guy, you call me and I'll see if I can find a place for you on my team. It might not be in Malibu and it might not be a lead designer position, but if I can fit you in, I will. That's how much I believe in you, Irie."

The tension in my shoulders seems to dissipate with her words and I find myself breathing a little easier all of a sudden.

I didn't come in here expecting anything from Kira.

Now I'll be leaving with a safety net.

"Are you sure?" I ask her.

"Two hundred percent," she says.

"Wow ... thank you ... so much."

"Of course, of course." Kira checks the Hermes Apple watch on her left wrist. "I've got a phone call in a few minutes, so if there's anything else you wanted to go over ...?"

"There is one thing," I say as I rise from the chair.

"Shoot." She stands.

"My boyfriend's mother is Camilla Masterson," I say.

Kira smiles. "Oh, Camilla. Right. I interned for her back in the day. We still keep in touch sometimes. What a small world!"

"Right." I gather my thoughts and a hard breath. I debated bringing this up at all but with my future at stake and Kira's generous offer, it seems like the right time. "Her son is Talon Gold, the quarterback for PVU."

"That's your boyfriend? Lucky ..."

"He's going to be playing football for Richmond, which is why I'm moving out east," I say. "But he almost didn't accept the contract ... and Camilla thought it had to do with me, so she asked me to break up with him. She told me if I didn't, she'd make a phone call to you and then she'd have me blacklisted."

The loudness of Kira's laugh sends a small startle to my heart. I wasn't expecting that kind of reaction. A second later, she dabs the tears from her eyes.

"Oh, Camilla," she says, chuckling and rolling her eyes. "She always had a flair for the theatrics. Anyway, I'm sorry if she scared you but rest assured, Camilla Masterson has no pull in this industry, not anymore, not since she married that developer and became a Real Housewife of Laguna Cove. And besides, I didn't get to where I am today by letting other people tell me what to do and who to hire."

Camilla walks around her desk, slipping her lithe arm around my shoulder as we head out of her office.

"Anyway, Irie, best of luck," she says. "And remember, if it doesn't work out with the quarterback, you call me."

CHAPTER 46

Talon

I SIGN my name a grand total of eleven times, sliding the completed contract across the table to Ira, who grabs it like he's Indiana Jones and it's some priceless crystal skull.

The energy is tense. No one has said more than a couple of words.

"There," I say, glancing around the packed restaurant. An hour ago, I asked them to meet me here. I didn't want them in my apartment again—that place is sacred ground, intended for good times—and good souls—only.

Ira folds the stack of papers neatly in half before tucking it into his inside jacket pocket.

Mom and Mark exchange looks, and I watch as he reaches for her hand across the table, giving it a squeeze as if to say, "We did it!"

I try not to think about how happy this makes them, instead focusing on what this means for Irie and me.

"We're so happy you came around," Mom says before

attempting to flag down a waiter, presumably for some *champs*. "You have no idea how proud Mark and I are of you, Talon. Truly. We can't wait to watch you play in Richmond. In fact, I was thinking maybe sometime this month we could take a trip out there and do a little house hunting? Something for you ... something for us ..."

"Just give us a budget, Tal. We'll try to stick to it." Mark wears the smuggest smirk I've ever seen, one that makes all his others pale in comparison.

Mark's real estate development empire is one of the biggest in all of Southern California. He doesn't need my money. He doesn't need handouts or a free McMansion—he feels entitled to it.

He thinks he earned it.

"Yeah, that won't be happening," I say before rising from the table.

"Talon, where are you going?" Mom asks, peering up at me with brows too Botoxed to furrow.

"I signed the contract. Now I'm out," I say, dropping the pen against the white tablecloth.

"But we're not finished yet," she says. "Let's talk about the move. Let's talk about the housing situation. All the fun stuff. I could even come out and help you decorate. Wouldn't that be fun?"

"Irie ... *Irie* will be decorating my home. *Our* home," I say. "So thanks, Mom. But no thanks."

Her joyous-yet-confused expression fades.

"Threatening her career, by the way? Class act," I say. "Way to go. You should be really fucking proud of yourself."

"Watch your tone," Mark chides, puffing his pathetic marshmallow chest.

"And you," I say. "Don't act like you weren't behind any of that. I'm sure you told her exactly what to say. You've always been good at that ... getting people to do what you want them to do. All you have to do is threaten something ... or someone ... they love and they do whatever you tell them to do. Right, Mark?"

Mom's attention snaps to Mark. "What is he talking about?"

"I'm sorry, but the two of you have no business being married," I say. "Mark, you're a goddamned user and a liar and Mom, you're too out of it to function half the time, the other half of the time you're acting like some puppet on a string, doing his dirty work. Honestly, I'm embarrassed for the both of you."

Ira sits in stunned silence, pretending to read his menu.

"Irie's moving east with me," I say. "We're starting a life together, without the meddling and the drama and the projecting and the manipulating. I will not be buying you a house, but you're welcome to watch the game on TV from the comfort of your own home."

I've never seen Mark and Mom so silent before.

"We want a little space," I say. "So maybe you can use this time apart from me to figure out your own shit. Mark, maybe you can push some of that excellence you're so obsessed with onto yourself. Maybe try being a better husband, how about that? Maybe take an interest in your daughters' lives and stop buying them shit to tell them you love them, maybe spend some actual time with them for once? And Mom, maybe take this time to start thinking about what it is you're really getting from this marriage. It's been a long time since I've seen you make a decision for yourself about anything."

Mom's gaze dips down to the napkin in her lap.

"Talon, that's enough." Mark's balled fist smacks against

the table, summoning a few dirty looks from the patrons around us.

"Anyway," I say, feeling light as air now that I've unloaded years' worth of their bullshit. "Ira, sorry you had to see all this. But before I go, if you so much as share another word about any of my contracts or career dealings, you're fired."

I leave the restaurant a new man in every sense of the word, the future suddenly looking brighter than I ever could have imagined.

CHAPTER 47

Irie

I'M WAITING at his apartment when he gets back from the gym Friday night, balanced on the edge of his kitchen island with the dopiest grin on my face.

He drops his gym bag at his feet, letting the door slam shut behind him, and he makes his way over, settling between my thighs, his hands on my waist.

He smells like soap and his hair is damp from the locker room shower and his hand is warm as it caresses my cheek. His thumb grazes along my bottom lip and a moment later, he kisses me soft and deep, burying his fingertips in the hair at the nape of my neck.

"I talked to Kira today," I say when we come up for air. "I turned down the job. We're doing this ..."

"How are you feeling?" he asks.

"Terrified. Mostly," I say. "But when I look at you, all of that goes away."

"Good. It should."

"How about you? How are you feeling?"

"Like a million fucking dollars." He kisses me again, pulling me against him before sliding me off the counter. A second later, he's carrying me back to his room, dropping me on the center of his bed. "Contract is signed. Assholes got a piece of my mind. And now I get to spend the night with my favorite girl. Doesn't get better than this."

"We need to find a place to live," I tell him.

"And we will," he says. "We'll find a home. Our first home. And you'll have free rein to do whatever you want to make it ours."

His left hand moves to the waistband of my shorts, un-popping the button before gliding the zipper down.

"I love you," I tell him as his mouth peppers a trail of kisses down my lower stomach.

I didn't think it was possible to feel every single emotion all at the same time, but this moment is proof that it's possible. I'm terrified about the future, exhilarated with hope, giddy with love, and hot with desire all at once.

Talon slides my shorts down my thighs, followed by my panties, and then he shoves his gym shorts down. A moment later, I'm pinned beneath him, his cock hot and throbbing against my sex.

"I love you more," he says as he buries his face into my neck, nibbling at my ears as his left hand veers between my legs. He teases my seam before circling my clit with his thumb. A second later, he slides two fingers inside me as my hips buck against him.

Suddenly I'm feeling anything but terrified.

He reaches over me, grabbing a condom from his nightstand, and I kiss his rounded shoulders, his skin still warm from his workout and the hot shower that followed.

I breathe him in—the man I adore more than anyone in this world. His musky, soapy scent. And I'm intoxicated.

Intoxicated with love, with hope.

They say good things are worth the wait—and while I didn't always consider Talon a good thing ... I'm so glad I waited before giving him a chance.

He was more than worth it.

CHAPTER 48

Talon

I HAND Irie a coffee when she gets to anthro Monday morning. It's the first day back after spring break and the lecture hall is packed with exhausted faces who don't want to be here—but not us.

Every day that passes is a day closer to graduation.

And the day after graduation, we're packing up our U-Haul and hitting the road.

"Aw, thank you." Irie takes her drink before unpacking her notebook and pen from her bag. "Did you get that link I sent you last night? The townhouse in Richmond?"

"I did."

"And? What'd you think?" she asks, taking a sip.

"I think you need to dream bigger, baby." I give her a wink before stealing a kiss.

"I don't think we should get carried away just yet. Oh! I wanted to show you something," she says before reaching into her bag and pulling out a hardback textbook. A moment later she flips to a page marked with a neon orange Post-It and hands it over. "Found this last night by pure chance."

"What's this?" I ask.

"It's a plan your father designed," she says. "I found it in one of my exteriors textbooks."

According to the blurb beside the picture, it's called Talon's Edge.

"I've never seen this one before," I say. "And I thought I'd seen them all."

"It was one of his last projects," she says. "Isn't it beautiful? Look at those clean lines and that symmetry. It's perfection."

I flip to the next page and find an image of the interior layout.

"I'm going to build this," I say, tracing my fingertips along the preserved image. "For us. In Richmond."

"Talon, this is eight thousand square feet ..."

"I don't care. This is it. This is our home," I say, nodding. "What do you think? You up for tackling a project like this?"

Her eyes widen. "It'd literally be a dream come true. But are you sure you want to do this?"

The overhead lights turn dark and the screen down front flicks to life. I turn to Irie, studying her face in the dark, the glimmer in her eyes, the sweet smile that claims her soft lips. All this time I thought nailing her would be the ultimate win, but now I know I was wrong.

"Yeah," I say. "I'm sure."

I'm going to marry this woman someday.

EPILOGUE

Irie

10 YEARS LATER...

I STAND on the balcony of our home on a balmy June afternoon, a drooling, teething baby Bette on my hip as I watch Talon toss a football to our seven-year-old son, Theo, in the backyard. The sun sets over Talon's Edge, painting the sky in warm shades of hibiscus and tangerine. It's nights like these, the simple and ordinary ones, that make me stop and think about how far we've come—and how all of this almost didn't happen.

Thank God for Talon's persistence.

You can give the man any goal in the world, and I swear, he'll make it happen.

It's a gift.

Sometimes I think he might be better at manifesting than football—though he's still pretty damn good at football.

One of the best in the league statistically, morally, or otherwise. Richmond just signed him to a new contract, this one worth an amount that makes me sick to my stomach when I think about it for too long. I guess when you lead your team to three Super Bowl victories in a row, they'll do whatever it takes to hang onto you. And don't even get me started on the sponsorships.

I don't know how he does it.

He's busier than ever and at the top of his game quite literally, but he still makes time for his family, and he's never once asked me to shutter my design business. And he wouldn't. He knows it's my passion. I've scaled back since we had our daughter, opting to be a bit choosier with my clients and the projects I'm willing to take on. Some days I'm spread paper-thin, other days I'm jubilant with exhaustion.

Talon has never once complained, never once asked me to scale back. He understands what it's like to be given a gift, to have a passion, and to be able to use it on your own terms.

"You want to swing, baby girl?" I say to Bette, bouncing her a little as I walk to the wooden playset several yards back, nestled in a thicket of blooming red peony bushes.

Bette smiles and instantly I think of her namesake, feeling a bittersweet sting in my center. I wish Bette would've been able to meet and hold my daughter. I can only imagine the kind of advice she would've been shelling out given her extensive experience raising girls (even if those girls were predominately strippers and one lame college student).

Talon gives me a wave before catching Theo's toss, and I blow them each a kiss.

A moment later, I secure baby Bette in her swing and give her a gentle push.

"Mom, watch!" Theo yells, grinning as he sprints across the grass and catches his dad's throw.

I cheer for him and his sister squeals.

Theo was a bit of a surprise originally. We weren't trying to get pregnant. In fact, I was on the pill, but some things tend to find their way when they're meant to be.

A couple of years after moving here, Talon and I eloped, tying the knot on a private beach along the Pacific, not far from Bette's house, surrounded by a few close friends. We didn't invite my aunt and uncle. Bette served as my maid of honor—and much to everyone's surprise, I took her up on her offer to throw me an epic bachelorette party.

Which she did.

Strippers and all.

Things with Talon's mom are better these days, especially since she left Mark. Their divorce was long and nasty and expensive, and she's still working through some of her own issues, but she agrees it was all worth it because now her relationship with her son is better than it's ever been.

She visits at least once a month, staying in the mother-in-law suite we had installed above the garage. She also travels with us during the off-season, when we're making our national rounds doing work on behalf of our Hero Ballers foundation. So far we've recruited a number of big names in the league and we're putting so much good into the world, making such a difference in ways we never expected.

We always dreamed big.

Turns out we needed to dream bigger.

So we did.

Earlier this year, Talon hired some private people finder group to locate my mom. It turns out she'd left her first commune sometime while I was in high school and took up with another, this one based out of Oregon and almost completely off the grid. A couple months after Bette was born, we took a trip out west to see her. I was apprehensive about going at first, not to mention a bit resentful at the fact that she made zero effort to be an ounce of the mother she should have been, but Talon said I needed to do this for me—for closure.

And maybe even for forgiveness.

He wasn't wrong.

The meeting was tear-filled and emotional, but watching her eyes light when she held her grandkids for the first time, watching how instantly enamored Theo was with his grandma made it all worth it.

One of these days she'll come out here, I'm sure. Someday when she's ready. Until then, I've made peace with accepting the fact that she wasn't able to be the mother I needed her to be—and that I'm not doomed to repeat her mistakes.

"All right," I say after another fifteen minutes of play time. "Time to head in and get baths and jammies."

Theo moans, throwing one more pass to his dad, and I scoop the baby into my arms. We head inside, our perfect little family, and make our way upstairs to run baths.

Moving to Richmond with Talon was, unquestionably, the best decision I've ever made in my life. It wasn't easy, throwing caution to the wind, walking away from a generous job offer, but I can't imagine my life with my husband and the two beautiful children we've made.

Sometimes you have to close your eyes and leap—and sometimes, if you're lucky, your best friend will be right there, holding your hand as you jump into the vast unknown together.

"Hey," Talon says, stopping me when we're outside the nursery.

"Yeah?"

"I love you," he says.

"That's all?" I ask, chuckling. For some reason, I thought he was going to tell me something else.

He leans down, kissing the top of Bette's head before kissing me. "That's all."

SAMPLE - THE MARRIAGE PACT

Synopsis

I was sixteen when I vowed I would never marry him.

We shook on it. Pinky swore. Even put it in writing and all but signed our names in blood.

It was the one and only thing we ever agreed on.

To the world, he's Prince Julian, Duke of Montcroix, second in line to the Chamont throne. Panty-melting accent. Royal charm. Hypnotic presence. Blindingly gorgeous. Laundry list of women all over the world who would give their firstborn for the chance to marry him. Most eligible bachelor in the free world …

But to me, he's nothing more than the son of my father's best friend—the pesky blue-eyed boy who made it his mission to annoy the ever-living hell out of me summer after summer as our families vacationed together, our parents oblivious to our mutual disdain as they joked about our "betrothal."

He was also my first kiss.

And my first taste of heartbreak so cataclysmic it almost broke me.

I meant it with every fiber of my soul when I swore I'd never marry him.

But on the eve of my 24th birthday, His Royal Highness had the audacity to show up at my door after years of silence and make a demand that will forever change the trajectory of our lives: "We have to break our pact."

Chapter 1

Emelie

"Em? There's a guy here to see you ..." My best friend Gillian stands in the doorway of my bathroom as I hover over the sink, scrubbing tonight's makeup from my face.

My feet ache from hours spent dancing in the most beautiful crystal-encrusted heels known to man, and my head has finally stopped spinning from the too-many-to-count top shelf cocktails. My body is in the process of thanking me for changing out of a skintight bandage dress and into jersey pajama pants and a cotton tank sans bra. I'm two point five seconds from crawling under the cool covers in my dark room and succumbing to a long, hard sleep.

After the year I've had, I needed tonight, but I have a feeling I'm going to be paying for it all day tomorrow.

"He probably has the wrong address." I press a dry

washcloth against my skin before moving for my moisturizer.

"Look, I admire your dedication to your skincare routine after a night on the town, but I'm serious. There's a guy at your door and he asked for you." Gillian bites her lip before continuing. "And, um, he's insanely, ridiculously hot."

I roll my eyes. Earlier tonight, a few of my friends were trying to hook me up with a dark-eyed stranger sitting at the end of the bar. It was every bit as awkward and embarrassing as it sounds, and he was clearly not having his best night. He just wanted to be alone in a room full of strangers. I get it. I've been there.

"Did Stacia tell him where I live?" I ask. "The guy from the bar?"

Gillian laughs through her nose. "No, no, no. The guy at your door is definitely *not* the guy from the bar."

I shoot her a look. I don't know what she's trying to pull, but I feel like I'm being set up.

"Did Hadley make a fake Tinder account in my name again?" I ask, one hand cocked on my hip.

Just because it's the eve of my twenty-fourth birthday and I've been going through a rough patch and a dry spell doesn't mean I'm in the mood to hook up with some random guy hand-selected by the most well-meaning yet least discerning friend in my group.

Gillian's hands lift to the air and she shrugs. "I don't know who this guy is, but he looks official."

"Official?"

"He's wearing a nice suit and he's got a security-looking guy with him."

"I'm so confused."

"You and me both." Gillian yanks me by the crook of my elbow and leads me down the hall and toward the front door. "So why don't you just see who he is and what he wants?"

"You realize how sketchy this sounds," I say.

"I do. That's why I'll have my phone out in case we need to call 9-1-1 ..."

"Reassuring." I sweep my hair off my neck and pile it onto the top of my head, securing it with a hair tie from my wrist, and then I take a deep breath before opening the door.

And then I hold that breath, deep in my lungs, until they burn.

"Hello, Emelie." A familiar sparkling blue gaze and signature half-smirk greets me. I'm tempted to slam the door in his face until I remind myself that he'd probably enjoy that too much.

"Julian," I say, hand gripping the edge of the door so hard my palm throbs. "What are you doing here?"

A man dressed in all black stands a couple of steps behind him, hands folded at his waist as he scans the area then returns his attention to his charge.

"I realize it's late," he says, an air of uncharacteristic remorse in his panty-melting voice. There are a million things I despise about this obnoxiously gorgeous specimen of a man, but his accent has never been one of them. Too casual to be the Queen's English. Too posh to be middle-American.

"Extremely," I say.

"But I'm afraid my matter is rather urgent."

I maintain my poise and poker face, keeping my vision trained on him despite the fact that the myriad of cocktails I enjoyed tonight are still working their way through my system.

"Would you mind if I came in and we chatted for a few moments?" he asks. His politeness is jarring, as is the pressed and tailored suit that covers his filled-in physique.

I run a quick calculation and determine that it's been almost eight years since I saw him last.

That's right.

It was the summer after I turned sixteen—a summer I'd do anything to forget.

I glance behind me and shoot Gillian a "help me out here" sort of look. She shoots me a quizzical look in return. She doesn't get it. And she wouldn't. I've never told her about *him* before.

"I have someone over," I begin to say. "Now's not really a good—"

"Hi, I'm Gillian." The door swings open wider, and Gillian takes the spot beside me, drinking in the handsome vision before us with zero shame. "We met a second ago when I answered the door."

She's drunker than I thought ...

"Em, you going to introduce me to your friend?" Gillian asks. "I find it odd that we've been best friends since our freshman year at Tulane and not once did you ever mention knowing ... this gentleman."

I study Julian's stunning physique from head to toe, noting the way he's filled out over the years. His jawline is sharper than before, his sandy brown hair perfectly coiffed, thick and windswept yet formal enough that he could waltz into a meeting at the United States embassy or grace a billboard in Times Square and no one would think twice.

"This is Julian," I say. "An old family *friend*."

"Right. From long ago. It's been ages, hasn't it, Em?" he asks. "Though sometimes it feels like it was yesterday."

"Yeah, it doesn't feel that way for me," I say. "Anyway, thanks for stopping by. We'll have to catch up another time."

"Emelie ..." Gillian whispers under her breath.

I realize I'm being rude, but was it not rude for him to show up unannounced at one o'clock in the morning after eight years of silence?

"Please, Emelie." Julian's rich accent fills my ears and makes my knees buckle ever so slightly. "A few moments of your time is all I'm asking for, then I'll be on my way."

I fold my arms across my chest as the cool night air wraps around me, sending a chill across my bare flesh, and I remember now that I'm standing in a white tank top, no bra, and sheer pajama pants—but it's the strangest thing: his eyes haven't once left mine.

He's being a perfect gentleman: charming, non-abrasive, and well-mannered.

But of course he is.

He wants something.

Giving into my piqued curiosity, I let him in.

"You have two minutes," I say as he and his man-in-black step across the threshold and into the small entryway of my townhome.

Gillian lingers for a second, fingers twitching at her sides, and then she mutters something before disappearing down the hall.

"Rafa, if you could excuse us for a moment?" Julian says to his bodyguard. At least, I assume it's his bodyguard. The man wears an intimidating straight face, not to mention he makes Julian look slight, and Julian is far from slight.

"There's a patio through there," I point to my left and Rafa heads to the sliding doors off my living room.

I'm afraid I don't have anywhere else for him to go. My townhouse is the definition of cozy and all the rooms sort of blur into one another—the entry blurs into the living room which blurs into a small dining area that becomes part of the kitchen. When I bought the place, the realtor called it "open concept." It sounded nice at the time, but after living here for a couple of years, I realize I forked over my entire life savings for a down payment on a glorified two-bedroom, one-bath shoebox. That farmhouse sink though ...

I'm pretty sure my entire home could fit into one of Julian's palatial bathrooms.

And *his* bathrooms are palatial ... given the fact that he lives in a literal palace.

Not that I've ever visited.

Our fathers were best friends who met as young boys at a private New England boarding school. After graduation, they kept in touch, and when they both married and started families, a tradition was born. Every summer, Julian and his parents would spend twelve weeks with us at our country home in Briar Cove, North Carolina. One big happy family ...

Despite the fact that Julian's father was a reigning king of a developed nation, he never acted like it around us. His one and only request was that we "treat him like anyone else." He didn't want to feel special. He wanted to feel like a regular guy with his regular wife and regular son enjoying a regular summer and spending time with their regular friends.

The last time I saw King Leo and Queen Marguerite was at my dad's funeral last year. The king was beside himself. The queen could barely utter more than a few condolences to my mother.

I busied myself with my younger sisters and wallowed in my own grief, though it didn't stop me from glancing around the funeral parlor every so often, half expecting to see Julian waltz in the door, but he never showed.

I was relieved.

I also hated him for it.

"Emelie." Julian narrows his gaze at me, my name melting off his tongue with finesse. "Why don't we have a seat?"

Rubbing my lips together, I glance at my humble living room with my used sofa and unfluffed pillows, the messy stack of glossy magazines, the half-burnt peony candle, and this morning's coffee mug, and I resist the urge to begin straightening up.

It's not that I care what Julian thinks, but I'd hate for anyone to get the impression that this is how I live, that my life is in shambles.

Today was a busy day, that's all. And when you live alone, sometimes you have better things to do than make sure your gossip magazines are stacked neatly and stowed away properly ...

"Still reading this rubbish, I see." He swipes an Us Weekly from the top of the stack.

"Still sticking your nose where it doesn't belong, I see." I take it from his supple, unworked hands and return it to the pile.

"Do they ever write about me here? In the States?" he asks. I don't know why he's playing coy. With an ego that size, I guarantee he knows exactly who writes about him and what they're saying. In fact, I wouldn't be surprised if he keeps an entire library of archived gossip articles in the Knightborne Palace library.

"Rarely," I lie. Two can play this game.

There's one magazine, Starwood, that writes about him incessantly. I'm pretty sure their editor-in-chief has a personal obsession with Julian. Last year I counted his chiseled likeness on no less than twenty-six covers, and I swear the story was the same recycled garbage about his on-again, off-again love, Princess Dayanara of Spain.

As much as I try to flip past those stories and convince myself that I couldn't care less what he's up to these days, I never can resist. It's like reading about an old high school nemesis, someone who bullied you, hoping they finally got their comeuppance.

Only as far as I can tell, he's yet to have his date with karma.

In fact, from what I've read, his life is pretty magical.

Trips to the Maldives, parties in Ibiza, private planes, a fleet of royal yachts at his leisure, women lined up everywhere he goes, throwing themselves at him.

Screaming.

Crying.

Professing their love.

If they only knew the real Prince Julian.

"Anyway, what is it you needed to talk to me about?" I ask, checking my watch and ignoring a text from Gillian that flashes across the screen. She's probably pacing my room, wondering what the hell is going on. And in all fairness, I never told any of my friends that I knew royalty.

That my first kiss was a prince.

That I gave my virginity to the future King of Chamont (more like he stole it).

After my sixteenth summer, it seemed irrelevant, and Julian wasn't anyone I wanted to bring up ever again.

"Do you remember that pact we made?" he asks. "The marriage pact?"

My stomach heaves and my blood runs cold.

Of all the things I expected him to bring up tonight, that was the last.

"If you're talking about the pact we made where we promised never to marry each other, then yes. I remember it. Clearly. In fact, it's the one thing from *that* summer that stands out most."

I've never told a single soul about our promise. I never wanted to have to explain it. I never wanted to explain *him*. Without the facts and details to accompany such a pact, it wouldn't make sense anyway.

I've had friends who've made marriage pacts of the mainstream variety—*if we're not married by thirty, we'll marry each other,* that sort of thing—but ours was ... unique.

And also necessary.

Our fathers were absolutely convinced that we were going to end up together one day, and our mothers used to throw around the word "betrothed" like candy at a parade with smiles on their faces as they were intoxicated off pricey white wine (and oblivious to our mutual disdain for one another that started long before either of us had so much as reached junior high).

After Prince Julian so callously and carelessly shattered my naive little teenage heart into a thousand-billion pieces, I had to make it clear in front of both of our families that a marriage between the two of us would never happen.

It was funny how quickly the word "betrothed" left our mothers' vocabularies after that.

"Good," Julian says. "I'm glad you remember it ... because we have to break it."

I start to reply but choke on my words, barely coughing out a simple, "What?!"

He can't be serious.

Julian smiles a devilish smile for all of two seconds before regaining his composure. He always did love getting reactions out of me.

"No," I say. "Absolutely not. Please tell me you didn't fly all the way to North Carolina to ask me to marry you."

"What if I did?"

"Then I'd say you're ...."

"What? I'm what?"

"Delusional?" I half-chuckle. "Insane? Arrogant? Mistaken? I would never marry you."

My hands fly through the air as I speak. I'm pretty sure I'm the one looking insane right now, but I'm too worked up to care.

Julian rakes his hand along his sharp jaw, exhaling. The tiniest bit of five o'clock shadow darkens his sun-kissed skin. I imagine he's been traveling all day and he's exhausted, but that isn't my problem.

I'm not the idiot who thought he could walk back into someone's life and expect her to say yes to his sorry excuse for a marriage proposal.

"I realize I'm asking the world of you, Emelie," he says, and I wish he'd stop saying my name. It's distracting coming from those full lips and soaked in that rich accent with his smooth cadence. "But I wouldn't come all this way and ask this of you if I weren't in dire straits."

"You're twenty-six." And the world's most eligible bachelor ... but I don't tell him that because he can't know that I've kept up on him all these years. "Why would you want to get married now? And to me? I don't even *like* you, Julian. What makes you think I'd even consider marrying you?"

My words are harsh, but the audacity of his request has me all kinds of stirred up and confused. I swear I'm feeling emotions I never knew existed before, and it's making my mind run a million miles per hour with contradicting thoughts.

I don't know what it is about first loves, but even the briefest ones leave their marks and the tiniest, most microscopic part of you can't un-love them, even if you can't stand them.

"You have every reason to feel the way you do, but please. Hear me out," he says.

I realize now that we've yet to take a seat. We're standing opposite each other, nothing but my cluttered coffee table separating us. I fold my arms over my chest, wishing I'd have thrown a cardigan over myself when I had the chance because how is he ever going to take me seriously when I'm standing here braless and indecent and barking at him like a crazy person who's been tossing back Belvederes all night?

"The monarchy is currently in jeopardy," he says. "In my father's age ... his beliefs are ... shifting, if you will. He's growing a bit extreme in his ways. Wanting to change things. The Chamontians, as you know, are a very outspoken people. They're not having it and quite frankly, neither am I. It's getting to the point where the media is making a mockery out of him and our country is becoming late-night talk show fodder."

"What does any of that have to do with you?" I ask. I vaguely recall reading a few articles here or there claiming King Lionel of Chamont is going senile in his old age, but beyond that I never gave them that much thought, writing them off like I do most gossip articles—as fictionalized entertainment.

"Our Parliament wants to do away with the monarchy completely," he says. "They feel it's a relic. A costly relic. And with my father acting out ... they feel the monarchy is a liability as well."

"Why don't you talk to him? Have him step aside?"

"Believe me, Emelie, I've tried that. It only makes things worse. He flies into these rages ..." his voice tempers into nothing. "We can't even have him examined by the royal physician. He's uncooperative and hostile toward everyone who comes into his path, my mother included."

A vision of King Leo at my dad's funeral last year comes to mind. Normally a stoic man with a round belly and a boisterous boom in his voice you can hear halfway across town, he was thinner, frailer, and quieter. Less hair. Lackluster blue eyes that had almost turned grey. I thought it was the loss of his best friend that was doing a number on him. Now I wonder if it was something more ...

"Our Parliament has the power to overthrow the monarchy and they're on the cusp of doing so, however, I've spoken with our prime minister, and she is willing to make an exception," he says. "She's willing to remove my father from power and replace him with a successor. However, the royal order, which spans back hundreds of years and dozens of generations, states that the successor must be married."

I roll my eyes. I can't help it. "If Parliament can overthrow your father, I'm sure they can change an outdated rule."

"I agree with you wholeheartedly," he says. "Unfortunately, I've had that conversation with our prime minister as well. Chamontian culture is steeped in tradition. This was a non-negotiable for them."

"Don't you have a cousin or something? An uncle?" I ask. I can't count how many times he confessed to me when we were younger that he had no interest in being king or running a country. He thought his father's job was boring and said he'd "sooner gouge my eyes out with a sterling silver caviar spoon."

"My father was an only child," he says. "I'm the only successor. I'm all they have."

"Your mother can't take over?"

"It doesn't work that way."

"It should."

"Right. It should. But it doesn't. And she wouldn't want to." He exhales, nostrils flaring. "Anyway, getting back to business, you're—"

"Wait." I lift a flattened palm. "Let me make sure I understand this. You need a wife, and the first person you think to ask is *me*?"

"Yes, Emelie," he says, jaw setting as he exhales through his perfect, straight nose. "I was just about to explain my rationale to you."

I silence my commentary and give him my full attention, but only because I'm dying of curiosity.

"My country, as you might know, has a rather complicated relationship with yours."

Fitting.

And also true.

"And I believe this could be a step in bridging that divide and changing ... *perspectives*. Public and personal." He pauses before locking eyes with me again. "To put it frankly, Emelie, Chamontians despise Americans, and from what I understand, the feeling is mutual."

"I don't think we should be generalizing, but I understand what you're getting at," I say. "That said, you're wasting your time. I'm ninety-nine percent sure you could walk up to any random American girl on the street and propose to her and she'll say yes. I mean, there's this whole Meghan Markle phenomenon now and there are a lot of girls dreaming of having royal weddings of their own, so ... lucky you."

"I don't want some random girl from the street, Emelie. I want you."

His words suck the air from my lungs, but not for long. "Do you hear yourself right now? How crazy you sound? You're not even making sense. I can't stand you, Julian. I would *never* marry you. And that's a promise I intend to keep."

I check my watch again before heading to the patio slider to let Rafa back inside.

"Our conversation is over," I say to them both before turning to Julian and escorting them to the door. "You came to ask a question. You got your answer. Good luck."

They leave, quiet. Dumfounded, probably. And I lock the door behind them, refusing to let myself watch through the peephole.

The instant they're gone, Gillian rushes down the hall, throwing questions at me faster than I can think to answer them, but I still have one of my own: why does he want *me*?

The man didn't just shatter my heart that summer, he obliterated it. It took me years to piece it back together and even then, it was never fully right after that. Never quite whole.

I meant it with every fiber in my soul when I swore I would never marry him.

I meant it then.

And I mean it now.

Chapter 2
Julian

"Julian." Emelie's mother, Delphine, greets me the next morning with open arms and wistful, glossy eyes. "It's been too long. How are you?"

We're standing in the sweeping entryway of the two-hundred-year-old Briar Cove, North Carolina colonial the Belleseaus have always called home, only instead of fresh flowers in cut crystal vases, imported rugs, and dazzling chandeliers, we're surrounded by stacked moving boxes.

Not only that, but I can't help but notice all of the light fixtures have been stripped from the walls, and in the parlor, a couple of gentlemen are hoisting up a velvet settee.

It turns out Mr. Belleseau had been struggling financially for several years before his untimely passing and nobody knew. His business was struggling, so he borrowed against the equity in his home, and because things were so tight, he let his life insurance policy lapse. When he died, he left behind a wife and three daughters, a mountain of debt, and an empty bank account.

Pierre Belleseau was a proud man. I can't say that I fault him for not wanting to worry his family. I'm sure every part of him believed he would reverse their situation all in due time, so there was no need to stress the others. How was he to know he was going to fall asleep behind the wheel after working a sixteen-hour day in the office?

"You have no idea how good it is to see you," Delphine says, still embracing me.

I had phoned her the other day and explained everything, including my plan to convince Emelie to marry me. We had a laugh about it at first, and then Delphine realized I was serious. Without pause, she gave me her blessing and told me how happy it would make Pierre to know that Emelie ended up with me. It was always his wish, she said, and then she informed me that Pierre always thought of me as the son he'd never had.

Delphine had also mentioned briefly over the phone that she was moving, but I didn't realize until now that she was taking all of their antique light fixtures as well. On second thought, I imagine she sold them for cash.

"How long will you be in town?" she asks. "Isabeau and Lucienne will be driving home from Duke tomorrow. They'll be here for the summer, though Isabeau has an internship in Charleston next month."

"I'm afraid I won't be in town more than a few more days," I say.

"When do you plan on visiting Emelie? You know it's her birthday today. I was planning on taking her out for brunch. You should join us!"

"I spoke with her last night, actually," I say. "I'm afraid she's not exactly open to my proposal. At least not yet."

I can't say that I blame her.

I'm not an imbecile—I knew I wouldn't be leaving there with a yes.

I just needed to plant the seed.

Now Delphine's going to water it for me.

"Excuse us," one of the movers says as he hoists a box onto his shoulder.

We step aside, and I manage to steal a glance into her kitchen, which is void of appliances, nothing but wooden cabinets and empty spaces where shiny metal objects used to reside.

We spent most of our summertime at their country house by the lake, but occasionally we'd head to their city house for a change of scenery or when Pierre had a work obligation he couldn't reschedule.

Delphine follows my gaze before realizing what it is I'm looking at, and then she covers her heart with a hand.

"My apologies. I don't mean to stare," I say.

"It's been hard," she says. "In *so* many ways ..."

"You don't have to say another word, Delphine."

Growing up, I never had extended family. Both of my parents were only children. I didn't have aunts or uncles or cousins. My grandparents weren't exactly the fun-loving, spoil-you-rotten type. They were typical stuffy royals and they passed when I was quite young. To be honest, I hardly remember them at all. If it weren't for the royal archives, they would be strangers to me.

The Belleseaus were the closest thing to extended family I ever had, and I loved them like family.

Still do.

It kills me to see Delphine shouldering all of this. I imagine she's selling this house piece by piece just to keep the lights on and maybe cover some of Luci and Isa's tuition. Pierre never would've wanted to see his family like this.

"Where are you going from here?" I ask Delphine.

"Brunch with Emelie," she says. "Remember? I told you it's her birthday today."

"No, I mean, where are you going to live?"

"Oh." Her shoulders fall and she peers out the open front door to the moving van parked on the browning grass of her once-immaculate front lawn. "I found a little apartment halfway between Durham and Emelie's place in Fayetteville."

For as long as I can remember, Delphine was a stay-at-home mother, and she relished in her role. She lived to take care of her family. It was her sole purpose, and her three daughters were her biggest pride and joy. Unfortunately her circumstances have left her much too young to retire much too inexperienced to land anything beyond an entry-level job.

"If Emelie marries me, your family will be royal-by-proxy," I say, half thinking out loud.

"I beg your pardon?"

"There will be a small stipend allocated for you and the other girls," I explain. "It's mostly to cover travel and other official engagements, but once I'm in charge, I can increase those allocations."

"Julian." Delphine's hand claps across her mouth. "You're incredibly thoughtful, but I couldn't take advantage of your generosity like that. It wouldn't be right."

"Nonsense. It wouldn't be right for me to turn a blind eye on your situation, Delphine." I take her hand. "It pains me to see you like this."

She swipes at a tear that falls from her left eye before tucking her chin against her chest.

"This is a very humbling moment for me, Julian," she says, voice broken as a breeze rustles her wavy blonde hair.

"What happened was a tragedy," I say. "But I would be honored to help. You're family to me. All of you. I want to help."

"Julian ..."

Delphine's eyes lock on mine, and I can't help but notice how hers match Emelie's fleck for fleck — green with the tiniest bits of gold if you look close enough. And they share the same sort of modern Grace Kelly poise. The way they move, the way they talk. The occasional flicker of a coy grin. My people would adore Emelie as their queen.

And secretly, I would too.

But for reasons of my own.

END OF SAMPLE.
Available Now!

ABOUT THE AUTHOR

Wall Street Journal and #1 Amazon bestselling author Winter Renshaw is a bona fide daydream believer. She lives somewhere in the middle of the USA and can rarely be seen without her trusty Mead notebook and ultra-portable laptop. When she's not writing, she's living the American Dream with her husband, three kids, the laziest puggle this side of the Mississippi, and a busy pug pup that officially owes her three pairs of shoes, one lamp cord, and an office chair (don't ask).

Winter also writes psychological suspense under the name Minka Kent. Her debut novel, THE MEMORY WATCHER, was optioned by NBC Universal in January 2018.

Winter is represented by Jill Marsal of Marsal Lyon Literary Agency.

Follow Winter on Instagram!

Like Winter on Facebook.

Join the private mailing list.

Join Winter's Facebook reader group/discussion group/street team, CAMP WINTER.

ABOUT THE AUTHOR

Wall Street Journal and #1 Amazon bestselling author Winter Renshaw is a bona fide daydream believer. She lives somewhere in the middle of the USA and can rarely be seen without her trusty Mead notebook and ultra-portable laptop. When she's not writing, she's living the American Dream with her husband, three kids, the laziest puggle this side of the Mississippi, and a busy pug pup that officially owes her three pairs of shoes, one lamp cord, and an office chair (don't ask).

Winter also writes psychological suspense under the name Minka Kent. Her debut novel, THE MEMORY WATCHER, was optioned by NBC Universal in January 2018.

Winter is represented by Jill Marsal of Marsal Lyon Literary Agency.

Follow Winter on Instagram!

Like Winter on Facebook.

Join the private mailing list.

Join Winter's Facebook reader group/discussion group/street team, CAMP WINTER.